The Lady With
The Red Shoes

ITA DALY

POOLBEG

First published in 1980 by
Poolbeg Press Ltd
Knocksedan House,
123 Baldoyle Industrial Estate,
Dublin 13, Ireland
This edition published 1995

The Publishers gratefully acknowledge the support of
The Arts Council.

A catalogue record for this book is available from the British Library.

ISBN 1 85371 456 9

Cover illustration by Laura Cronin
Cover design by Poolbeg Group Services Ltd
Printed by The Guernsey Press Ltd,
Vale, Guernsey, Channel Islands.

Contents

With acknowledgements to *The Irish Press 'New Irish Writing'*, *Cara*, *The Irish Times*, *Short Story International*, *The Irish Woman*, *Threshold*, *Modern Irish Love Stories (Pan Books)*, *Best Irish Short Stories (Paul Elek Ltd.,)* and *The Critic (U.S.A.)* where some of these stories previously appeared. 'Virginibus Puerisque' and 'The Lady With The Red Shoes' won Hennessy Literary Awards and 'Compassion' won The Irish Times Short Story Competition, 1975.

This book is one of a series devoted to the modern Irish short story.
Ireland's contribution to the short story is world famous, but much of the best work both of the acknowledged masters and of the new hands is either out of print or has never been published in book form.
The aim of this series is to make that work generally available.

The Lady With The Red Shoes

The West of Ireland, as every schoolboy knows, is that part of the country to which Cromwell banished the heretical natives after he had successfully brought the nation to heel. Today, it is as impoverished and barren as ever it was, bleak and lonesome and cowering from the savagery of the Atlantic which batters its coastline with all the fury that it has gathered in over three thousand miles. But the West of Ireland can also be heartbreakingly beautiful; and on a fine April morning with the smell of gorse and clover filling the air and the bees showing the only evidence of industry in a landscape that is peopleless as far as the eye can see — on such a morning in the West of Ireland you can get a whiff of Paradise.

It is an irony which pleases me mightily that we as a family have such a strong attachment to the West. Our ancestors, you see, came over with Cromwell, foot soldiers who fought bravely and were rewarded generously and have never looked back since. And every Easter we leave Dublin and set out westwards where we spend a fortnight in McAndrews Hotel in North Mayo. It is a family tradition, started by my grandfather, and by now it has achieved a certain sacredness. Nothing is allowed to interfere with the ritual, and so when I married Judith one April day, some twenty-five years ago, it seemed quite natural that we should spend our honeymoon there. We have gone there every Easter since and if Judith has found it somewhat dull on occasion, she accepts gracefully a period of boredom in the knowledge that it gives me so much pleasure, while I in turn have been known to accompany her to Juan-les-Pins. An experience which, however, I have not been foolish enough to repeat.

McAndrews is one of the puzzles of the world. Built on the outskirts of Kilgory, looking down on the hamlet and on the sea, it dates back to the late nineteenth century. A large, square house, red-bricked and turreted, it is a reminder of the worst excesses of the Gothic revival, and every time I see its monstrous outline, lonely on the hill, my heart bounds and my pulse quickens. Nobody knows whether it was there before Kilgory and the village grew up around it or whether Kilgory was there first. But certainly it seems an odd place to have built a hotel, miles from a town, or a church, or even a beach. It is situated on a headland overlooking the Atlantic, but the cliffs are so steep and the sea so treacherous here that there is neither boating nor swimming available. Strange to build a hotel in such a place, stranger still that there have been enough eccentrics around to keep it in business for almost a century. My father, as a boy, used to arrive by train. The main line ran from Dublin to Westport and from there a branch line went to the hotel — not to Kilgory mark you, but to the actual hotel grounds. 'Any guests for McAndrews?' the porters used to shout as one disembarked at Westport and was ushered onto a toy train with its three or four first-class carriages, to be shunted along the fifteen miles and deposited a stone's throw from the grand front door of McAndrews with its noble stone balustrade.

The toy station is still there, although nowadays the guests arrive by motor. I am always glad when I see my Daimler disappearing into the cavernous garages, and most of the other guests seem to experience a similar sense of relief, for though they arrive in motor-cars, they continue thereafter on foot and the grounds and environs are delightfully free of petrol fumes. We are of a kind, McAndrews clientele, old-fashioned, odd perhaps; some would say snobbish. Well, if it is snobbish to exercise one's taste, then I admit that I am a snob. I do not like the bad manners, the insolence of shop assistants and taxi-drivers which passes for egalitarianism in this present age; I resent chummy overtures from waiters who sometimes appear to restrain themselves with difficulty from slapping one on the back. I am irritated by cocktail bars and at a loss in the midst of all that bright and fatuous chatter. I like peace and quiet and reserve in my fellow-man — decent reserve, which appears to be the *raison d'etre* of McAndrews. I know most of my fellow-guests' names — like me they have been coming here since they were children — yet I can rest assured that when I meet any of them again in any part of the hotel, I shall be spared all social intercourse apart from a civil word of greeting. Such respect for dignity and personal privacy is hard to come by in commercial establishments these days.

This year, Judith was ill and did not accompany me. To say that she was ill is something of an exaggeration, for if she had been, I would certainly not have left her. But she was somewhat under the weather, and as her sister was in Dublin from London, she decided to stay there with her while I went to Mayo alone. In truth, I was somewhat

7

relieved, for I am only too aware of how difficult it must be for Judith, gay and outgoing, to be married to a dry stick like myself all these years. I am glad when she gets an opportunity to enjoy herself and I had no doubt that Eleanor and she would be much happier without my inhibiting presence. Still, I was going to miss her, for like many solitary people I am very dependent on the company of those few whom I love.

But the magic of McAndrews began to re-assert itself as soon as I got down to breakfast the first morning and found Murphy, with his accustomed air of calm and dignity, presiding over the dining-room. Murphy has been head waiter here for over thirty years now, although I always see him more as a butler, a loyal family retainer, rather than as a smart *maître d'hôtel*. His concern for each guest is personal and his old face is suffused with genuine pleasure when he sees you again each year. He came forward to greet me now. 'Good morning, sir.'

'Good morning, Murphy. Nice to see you again.'

'And you, sir, always such a pleasure. I'm sorry Mrs Montgomery will not be with us this year, sir?'

'Afraid not.'

'Nevertheless, I hope you will have a pleasant stay. May I recommend the kippers this morning, sir? They are particularly good.'

Such exchanges would be the extent of my inter-course with the world for the next fortnight — formal, impersonal, remote, and totally predictable. I have always found it a healing process, part of the total McAndrews experience, helping one to relax, unbend, find one's soul again.

I quickly re-established my routine, falling into it with the ease and gratitude one feels on putting on again an old and much-worn jacket. Breakfasts were latish but hearty, then a walk as far as the village and back. Afterwards an hour or two spent in the library in the delightful company of Boswell, a man to be enjoyed only in leisured circumstances — I never read him in Dublin. Lunch and an afternoon in a deck-chair in the gardens, looking out to sea, dozing, dreaming, idling. After dinner another walk, this time more strenuous, perhaps two miles along the coast road and then back to McAndrews for a final glass of port followed by early bed with a good detective novel. The bliss of those days is hard to convey, particularly the afternoons, when it never seemed to rain. I would take my deck-chair and place it in a sheltered spot and sit, hour upon hour, and watch the Atlantic at its ceaseless labours. I'd watch as the light changed — from blue to green and from green to grey — until an occasional sea-gull would cut across my line of vision and I would raise my eyes and follow its soaring flight to the great vault of heaven. A couple of afternoons like that and things were back in perspective. The consciousness of one's encroaching age, the knowledge that one is regarded as a has-been, became less painful, and there, on the edge of the Atlantic, a peace began to make itself felt.

But then I have always been out of step with the world and even as a young man McAndrews was a retreat, a haven for me. However as I grow older and my unease increases, McAndrews becomes more precious. Here I can escape from all those aggressive young men with their extraordinary self-confidence and their scarlet-nailed women and their endless easy chatter. My son, Edward, who is married to a beautician — a profession which, I am assured, has some standing in this modern world — this son of mine tells me that my only problem is that I am a nasty old snob. This apparently puts me completely beyond the pale, and he views me as a pariah, almost as someone who should be put down. But we are all snobs of one variety or other, and what he really means is that my particular brand of snobbery has gone out of fashion. He has working-class friends and black friends, but no stupid friends; he would not dream of spending his holidays in such a bastion of privilege as McAndrews, but then neither would he think of going to the Costa Brava; he drinks pints of Guinness but abhors sweet wine. And he tells me that the difference between us is that he has discernment and that I am a snob.

The generation gap is what any modern sociologist would inelegantly and erroneously call it, for, as I have said, there has always been as big a gap between me and most of my own generation as there is between me and Edward's. It is a painful sensation, constantly feeling that the time is out of joint, although as I sit sipping sherry in McAndrews, in the pleasant expectation of a good dinner, I can laugh at my own foolishness and that of my son, and indeed, at the general idiocy of the human animal. This is what makes McAndrews so dear to me, but it is also what makes each leave-taking so difficult. I grow increasingly apprehensive before every return to the world, and as this holiday drew to a close and I finally sat waiting for dinner on the last evening, I was aware of my mounting nervousness and depression. I decided to console myself with that nectar of so many ageing men — a bottle of vintage claret. Now as I sought Murphy's advice, I ignored, with unaccustomed recklessness, both the price and the knowledge that if I drank the whole bottle, I would undoubtedly spend a sleepless night. There were worse things than insomnia.

By dinner-time the light had changed outside and a soft blue opacity was flooding in from the Atlantic through the great windows of the dining-room. This is the Irish twilight, most beautiful of times and that part of the day I missed most during those few years I spent in West Africa as a young man. It is a time that induces a half-wilful melancholia — helped no doubt by the glass in one's hand — and in McAndrews they respect this mood, for the curtains are never drawn nor the lights switched on until darkness finally descends. As I moved through the flickering pools of yellow light — for there were many diners already present and many candles lit — I was struck again by the solemnity of the room. Years and years of ritual have given it a churchlike quiet, a hint of the ceremony and seriousness with which eating is invested by both guests and staff. I took my usual seat against the wall, facing out towards sea, and as Murphy murmured, priest-like, over the wine, we were both startled by a raised and discordant voice. 'Waiter, come here please.'

Together we turned towards the voice, both acutely conscious of the solecism that had been committed in referring to Murphy as 'Waiter'. The offender was sitting about six feet away at a small table in the middle of the room. It was an unpopular table, unprotected, marooned under the main chandelier, seldom occupied except when the hotel was very busy. I guessed now that some underling, flustered by the novelty of the situation, had forgotten himself to such an extent as to usher this person to it without first consulting Murphy. And the arrival of this new diner *was* a novelty. She was not a resident, which was odd in itself, for

11

McAndrews has never been the sort of place to seek out a casual trade; then she was alone, unescorted, a sight which was not only odd, but simply not done: ladies, one feels, do not dine alone in public. But the most striking thing of all about our newcomer was her appearance. She was in her fifties, maybe sixty, with hair and dress matching, both of an indeterminate pink. She wore spectacles which were decorated with some kind of stones along the wings. These shone and sparkled as she moved her head, but no more brightly than her teeth, which were of an amazing and American brightness. She flashed them up at Murphy now, and as he shied away from their brilliance, I could see that for once he was discomposed. But Murphy is a gentleman and within seconds he had himself again in hand. Stiffening his back, he bowed slightly in the direction of the teeth. 'Madam?' he enquired, with dignity.

'Could I have a double Scotch on the rocks, and I'd like a look at the menu.' Her voice had that familiarity which so many aspects of American life have for Europeans who have never even crossed the Atlantic. I don't think I have ever met an American, but I have a great fondness for their television thrillers, and I immediately identified the voice as a New York voice, tough New York, like so many of my favourite villains. Proud of my detective work, I sat back to listen.

The whiskey had appeared with that speed to which we McAndrews guests are accustomed, and if Murphy disapproved of this solitary diner, his training was too perfect to even suggest it. He hovered beside her now, solicitously, as she studied the menu, and as she turned it over and turned it back again I noticed her face grow tight and ap-

12

prehensive. I should say here that McAndrews does not have a menu in the usual commercial sense of that word. Mrs Byrne, who has been cooking there for the past thirty years, is an artist, and it would offend her artistic sensibility, and indeed equally displease the guests, if she were asked to produce the commonplace, vast à la carte vulgarity that one finds in so many dining places today. For festive occasions she will prepare a classic dish in the French tradition, and otherwise she keeps us all happy cooking simple but superb dishes using the local fish and meat and the vegetables which grow a couple of hundred yards away. She is a wonder certainly, but I can perfectly understand that one used to the meaningless internationalism of the modern menu might find Mrs Byrne's hand-written and modest proposals something of a puzzle. One would look in vain for the tired Entrecôte Chasseur or the ubiquitous Sole Bonne Femme in this dining-room and be somewhat at a loss when faced with the humble, boiled silverside of beef followed by stewed damsons with ginger.

I could see that this was precisely the position in which our lady diner now found herself. She toyed with the piece of paper and looked up helplessly at Murphy. Murphy coughed encouragingly behind a genteel hand and began, 'Perhaps Madam, I could recommend tonight the –'. But she gathered her shoulders together and threw back her head. 'No, you could not, waiter. I know exactly what I want.' Her voice had taken on an added stridency. 'I want a fillet mignon with a green salad. Surely a place like this can produce that – huh?'

'It is not on the menu, Madam, but certainly if that is what you require, we can arrange it.' I thought I noticed a hint of disapproval in Murphy's silky tones.

'Yeah, that's what I want. Nothing to start and I want the steak medium-rare, and I mean medium-rare. All you Irish overcook meat.'

I thought for a moment that Murphy was going to lose control, that years of training and polish would at last begin to give way before this latest onslaught of rudeness, but again he recovered himself. For a second he paused over his order and then looked up again and said, still politely, 'And to drink Madam, would you like something?' The lady looked at him, genuinely puzzled as she held up her whiskey glass. 'I've gotten it already — remember?' It was now Murphy's turn to look puzzled and I could see him struggling mentally before the implication of her remark became clear to him. This extraordinary person intended to drink whiskey with her fillet mignon!

As I watched my fellow-diner I wondered how on earth she had ever found her way to McAndrews. It was not a fashionable spot, not the sort of place that attracted tourists. There was a hideous motel only ten miles away, much smarter than McAndrews, flashing neon lights, full of Americans, supplying what they called an ensemble for the gratification of their guests. Surely this woman would have been much more at home in such a place? But as I studied her, I began to realize that this strange creature was actually impressed by McAndrews. I was sure now that she hadn't accidentally happened upon it as I had at first surmised, but that for some unknown reason she had chosen it deliberately. And I saw too that her apparent rudeness was no more than awkwardness, an effort to hide her awe and inexperience in such surroundings. My daughter-in-law — the beautician — when she visited me here once

14

gave a display of genuine rudeness, authentic because it was based on contempt, for Murphy, for me, for our kind of world. She shouted at Murphy because she saw him as an inefficient old fogey. But he didn't impinge at all on her world and was only a nuisance to her because he did not mix her cocktail in the correct proportions. This woman however was different, although I saw that Murphy didn't think so — indeed whereas he was prepared to make excuses for Helen, as one of the family, I could tell that he had put up with as much as he was going to from an outsider. As the waiter placed the steak in front of her, Murphy approached, disapproval in every line of his stately person. 'Medium rare, as you required,' he said, and even I, sitting some distance away, drew back from the sting of his contempt.

Other guests were taking notice now, attracted perhaps by Murphy's slightly raised voice, a unique occurrence in this dining-room. I could feel a current of mild disapproval beginning to circulate and I saw that the lady was noticing something too. She was looking discomfited but bravely she took up her knife and fork and tucked in her chin. I was beginning to admire her pluck.

Decency demanded that I leave her some privacy to eat so reluctantly I looked away. Soon, I was glad to see, the other guests lost interest in her, and when after a safe interval I glanced back at her table, she had finished her meal and was wiping her mouth with an air of well-being and relaxation. It must have been a satisfactory fillet mignon. When Murphy brought the menu again, she actually smiled at him. 'No, no,' she said waving it away, 'nothing more for me. We women have to watch our figures — eh?' And as she glanced at him archly, I thought for

15

an awful moment that she was going to dig him in the ribs. Murphy looked at her coldly, making no effort to return her smile. 'Very well, Madam.' The words hung between them and as she sensed his unfriendliness, indeed hostility, the smile, still awkward upon her lips, became transfixed in an ugly grimace. 'I guess you'd better bring me another Scotch.' Defeat was now beginning to edge out defiance in her voice. She grasped her drink when it arrived, and gulped it, as a drowning man gulps air. This seemed to steady her somewhat and taking another, slower sip, she drew out a cigarette from her bag and lit it. It was then that she discovered, just as Murphy was passing on his way towards my table, that there was no ashtray. 'Excuse me,' she sounded embarrassed, 'could you bring me an ashtray please?' Murphy turned slowly in his tracks. He looked at her in silence for fully five seconds. 'I am sorry, Madam,' — and it seemed to me now that the whole dining-room was listening to his even, slightly heightened tones — 'I am sorry, but our guests do not smoke in the dining-room.' In essence this is true, it being accepted among the guests that tobacco is not used in here — a measure of their consideration for each other as smoke fumes might lessen someone's enjoyment of an excellent meal. I thoroughly approve of this unwritten rule — it seems to me to be eminently civilized — but I know well that on occasion, people, newcomers for example, have smoked in McAndrews dining-room, and Murphy, though perhaps disapproving, has never demurred. I looked at him now in amazement and maybe he caught my expression of surprise, for he added, 'Coffee is served in the blue sitting-room, Madam, there are ashtrays there. However, if you'd prefer it, I can —'

The woman stood up abruptly, almost colliding with Murphy. Her face and neck were flooded with an ugly red colour and she seemed to be trying to push him away. 'No, not at all, I'll have the coffee,' and she blundered blindly towards the door. It seemed a long, long journey.

I finished my cheese and followed her thoughtfully into the sitting-room. All evening something had been niggling me, something about that voice. I have a very sensitive ear I believe — I am rather proud of it — and although, as I had noticed, this woman spoke with an American accent, there was some underlying non-American quality about it. Something familiar but different about those vowels and th's. Now as I sat and lit my cigar, I realized what it was — it was so obvious that I had missed it until now. Her voice, of course, was a local voice, a North Mayo voice with that thick and doughy consistency that I was hearing around me since I had come down. It had become Americanized, almost completely so, but to my ear its origins were clear. I could swear that that woman had been born within ten miles of this very hotel.

We both sipped our coffee, the tinkle of coffee-spoons falling between us. I watched her as she sat alone, isolated and tiny in the deep recess of the bay window, looking out at the darkening gardens. Beyond, there were still some streaks of light coming from the sea, and I knew that down below on the rocks the village children would be gathering their final bundles of seaweed before heading off home to bed. The seaweed is sold to the local factory where it is turned into fertilizer of some kind and the people here collect it assiduously, sometimes whole families working together, barefooted, for the salt water rots shoe-leather. Even the little ones often have hard and calloused feet, sometimes with ugly cuts. Life is still hard in the West of Ireland. I looked across at my lady — *her* feet were encased in red high-heeled shoes with large platform soles. Her face, as she gazed out unseeing, was sad now, sad and crumpled-looking. I recalled again her voice, and as we sat there, drinking our coffee, I suddenly knew without any shadow of doubt what she was doing there. I knew *her* intimately — her life was spread out in front of me. I could see her as a little girl, living nearby in some miserable cottage. Maybe, when I was out walking as a child with my Mama, I had even passed her, not noticing the tattered little girl who stood in wonder, staring at us. McAndrews must have been a symbol to her, a world of wealth and comfort, right there on the doorstep of her own poverty-stricken existence. Perhaps she had even worked in the hotel as a maid, waiting to save her fare to America, land of opportunity. And in America, had she been lonely, frightened by that alien place, so different from her own Mayo? Had she wept herself to sleep many nights, sick for a breath of home? But she had got on, sent money back, and always, all those years, she had kept her dream intact: one day she would return home to Kilgory, a rich American lady, and she would go into McAndrews Hotel, not as a maid this time but as a guest. She would order a fine dinner and impress everyone with her clothes and her accent and her wealth.

She sat now, a rejected doll in her pink dress and red shoes, for tonight she had seen that dream disintegrate like candy-floss. I wanted to go to her, to tell her, explain to her that it didn't matter any more — the world itself was disintegrating. She should realize that places like McAndrews weren't important any longer, people only laughed at them now. She had no need to be saddened, for she, and all those other little Irish girls who had spent their days washing other people's floors and cooking other people's meals, they would inherit the earth. The wheel had come round full circle.

Of course I didn't approach her. I finished my coffee and went straight to bed thinking how the world is changing, my world, her world. Soon McAndrews itself will be gone. But for me, this landscape has been caught forever — caught and defined by its heroine, the lady with the red shoes. Of course, you, on reading this, are going to see me as a sentimental old codger, making up romantic stories about strangers, because I am lonely and have nothing better to do. But I know what I know.

Virginibus Puerisque

Rome is best approached by road and best of all approached from the North, Liza felt. Your starting out point should be Florence. Leave Florence and journey down the Autostrada Del Sol. You will whizz along the smooth efficient highway, so much at odds with the countryside beyond. You will leave behind the soft voluptuousness of Tuscany and savour the approaching thrift of the Umbrian landscape. And thus you will be prepared gradually for the city itself. For Rome.

That was how Liza had first seen Rome. But this time as she stood in Rome's international airport and looked around at its smart anonymity, she could feel only dullness. She waited behind Stephen in the queue for the Customs and wondered if it was because of their comparative newness that airports were always so characterless. She was uneasy and apprehensive, because she realised, guiltily, that what she had been looking forward to about her honeymoon was the fact that it was being spent in Rome. There would be no first-night raptures of course. June, honeymoon. Whimsically she wondered about this kind of lyricism. She found it appealing though she realised that to her its appeal could only be academic. 'Here I am in Rome,' she thought, 'with a new husband, new suitcases and new underwear, and I never felt so

20

silly in my life.' Did she look as silly as she felt? She caught a glimpse of herself in a mirror opposite. The large picture-hat was regular honeymoon gear in Dublin. Like the honeymoon itself, it was felt that one was not decently wedded without it. Oh well, stop moaning, girl. Enjoy it. Play the game. Where's the much-lauded sense of humour? Coyly she looked at the Customs official, and when she caught his glance, modestly she lowered her eyes. She wished she could have managed a blush. He laughed, delighted with this obvious bride, who behaved in such a seemly, almost Latin manner. Stephen smiled too, pleased that his bride was being admired.

Stephen Hero she called him. She looked at him now, appraising him. She had a predilection for handsome men, and Stephen looked very handsome today. He had an air of distinction about him, a fine dry intelligence emanating from him which somehow diluted his physical handsomeness, preventing it from becoming brash. All this and beddable too. Liza pulled herself up, displeased with herself. One ought not to analyse thus a new husband, with such a mixture of off-handed wryness. Well, never mind. Maybe tonight they would make love in a frescoéd room, overlooking a cool courtyard, dusty and quiet, while Rome throbbed outside. She felt her excitement grow.

They boarded the airport bus. The heat was oppressive and she welcomed it, wallowed in its heaviness. Her smart linen suit was limp and stained with perspiration at the armpits. Her hair was sticky and she knew that no number of cool showers or glasses of icy lemonade would revive her. She would grow more and more limp until finally her very nerves would become blunt and her mind, like her body, would accept and submit. Rome had the ability to sap one's being like no other city she knew — to leave one drained, void, so satisfyingly empty.

Rome, the slattern, spread herself in front of them. Her appalling monuments, her decaying churches, her vulgar fountains were revealed mercilessly in the brilliant sunshine. She laughed back, careless of her appearance, frank, friendly, generous. Thank God they hadn't chosen Florence, Liza thought, prim and classical, full of echoes of John Milton and his puritan breed. Stephen Hero sat looking out the window. He held her hand and Liza realised that only Stephen Hero could hold one's hand in such heat, with no suggestion of clamminess. Again she marvelled at her own good taste, in men as in suitcases: Stephen Hero and brown pig-skin suitcases — only the nicest of sensibilities could achieve such a combination. 'Roma, I love you.' Liza mouthed the words.

She had begun to recognise some of the streets now as they crossed over the Ponte Sixto. The buildings had a grey still quality. The leaves of the trees that lined the Tiber were dust laden and ready to fall off under their weight. The water of the river was sluggish and oily. Liza looked with affection. Absurd to feel this affection for a city that one had only visited once for a fortnight, four years ago. She felt the need to explain, to herself as much as to Stephen.

'Oh, Stephen,' she said, 'I'm so happy to be in Rome. And you are *so* kind to agree to our coming here when you know how much it means to me. It was my first taste of Europe, you know, of being away from home. Jonny and I spent a fortnight here. We hadn't a penny. We stayed in the youth hostel up on the Via Caligula. And we walked miles every day to our lunch . . .'

'I know, darling,' Stephen said gently, 'you have told me before, you know.'

'Oh, I'm sorry, I'm being such a bore . . .'

'You know you can never bore me.'

She felt a rush of affection for him. He was so honest about his love for her.

'It was such a special holiday.'

Liza could almost feel again the texture of the happiness she had experienced four years ago. 'Jonny and I, well, you know how close we have always been. I suppose it was because there were only the two of us. My father gave me the money to mind — he knew Jonny — and every morning after breakfast we'd see how many lira we could afford to spend that day. And we learned the Italian for ice-cream — *gelati*, and where is — *dove é*, and thank you — *grazie*. I wore jeans for the whole fortnight. I brought them with me again — I'm going to change when we get to the hotel.'

Their room was indeed beautiful. Shuttered against the sunlight, gold strips of brightness lightened the green of the carpet. Below, from a great distance, came the hum of the Roman traffic. The bed was huge and ornate, and over it, in the middle of the ceiling, was a group of cherubs, their rounded cheeks cracked with age. As Liza stood under the shower in the adjoining bathroom, she had the absurd feeling that she could recognise a familiar quality in the Roman water as it fell on her back. In the youth hostel, there had been one shower in the women's quarters — the rest were out of order. Jonny had wanted her to use the fountains — 'Go on, don't be so illogical. It's water going to waste.' He had been great at getting lifts

23

too, Jonny, and he had encouraged her mild flirtations with the drivers, highly amused that anyone should want to flirt with his sister. He was proud of her though. Said she shared the family distinction. 'My soror,' he would roar at the drivers, eccentrically convinced that all Italians must speak Latin as well as Italian.

Liza returned to the bedroom and took out her jeans. She fitted them on, but they would not close over her hips. Two years of love-making had broadened those hips. They were virgin hips the last time she was in Rome. Boyish. Smart, economical. She felt a stab of nostalgia — for what? For the freedom of being a virgin in Rome, with her brother, when her future was so unknown and uncertain as to be full of magic.

Stephen came from the shower and threw the towel on the floor. She looked at him with interest and detachment. Stephen's body was compact and vibrant. The ripple of the muscles under the milky skin had always reminded her of Michelangelo's 'David'. In fact, now that she came to think of it, the first time she had seen Stephen on the beach at Carraroe, he had been christened 'David' by Jonny. The family had taken a cottage there that year and Jonny and herself were walking down the little road to the shore. He was sulking because she had refused to give him half-a-crown he wanted for his morning pint. Suddenly he nudged her, his sulky face brightening. 'Hey,' he said, 'look over there — a real live "David".' He had pronounced it in the Italian way, as they had learned to do in Florence the year before. They had both been bored by Tuscan perfection, but still she had wanted to stay on, going back day after day to gaze at the marble perfection in the hallway of the Academia. He had

24

grown impatient with her. 'Art my eye; it's sex, my girl, that's what it is, nothing more. And it's all right for you, but I'm left with nothing but those cow-eyed madonnas.'

He pointed out Stephen on the beach that day in Carraroe. 'Now you can recoup some of those lost lira. Off and wiggle your hips at him. He might take you out for a jar and then you could lend me the half dollar.'

Well, she had wiggled them. But that had been four years ago.

'Fatty, who are you trying to fool?' Stephen came over and put his hands on Liza's hips. 'Take them off,' he whispered, beginning to pull them down. She moved away gently, controlling her irritation. Stephen didn't usually mistime things so badly. Energetically she began to unpack. 'Come on, darling, get dressed. We'll have an early dinner, and then an early night.' She tried to put warmth into her voice as she said it. As she got dressed she became conscious of her own ambivalence. What was wrong with her? Why the hell was she feeling like this? She realised that she had been narked with Stephen since they arrived at the airport. He was, somehow, an intrusion. Ironic thought, that, on your honeymoon. She smiled.

'I'll tell you what,' she turned towards him, taking his hand. 'Could we eat at Mario's, you know, the place I told you about. It's not very far away, and I'd really love to.'

Stephen never sulked. With grace and tolerance he indulged her, straightening a new olive tie with precision and kissing her with the friendliness and lack of warmth that he realised the moment demanded.

They left the hotel arm-in-arm and in the

softening light walked the quarter of a mile to Mario's. It didn't seem to have changed at all in the last four years. It was still dark and small and surprisingly cool. Wine from Orvieto lay in barrels behind the bar. The smell of garlic mixed with cooking tomatoes. The bread lying in the baskets was coarse and wholesome. The clients were mostly family parties, slightly shabby, with one or two groups of students.

'You like it, Stephen?' Now that she had been pleased, Liza wanted Stephen to share her enthusiasm. The meal was solid and heavy as she remembered them, soup and pasta, chicken and salad. The salad dressing, like the water of the shower, had a familiar tang. They drank the harsh wine of Orvieto and grew gay and closer than they had been all day. The wine, red and thick, sent currents of ease and satisfaction coursing through their bodies. The enervating effect created an intimacy between them, as their two bodies sank in lassitude together. 'Let's have another glass of wine, and then go back. Remember, I said an early night.' This time Liza had no difficulty putting warmth into her voice. She was greatly relieved that her strange reluctance of the afternoon had disappeared. Now she wanted desperately, and suddenly, to go to bed with her husband. Her face grew red with passion, blood rushing to it as she looked at him across the table. His eyes met hers and locked, then broke away again. It was a glance of animal awareness, subtle yet blatant, a glance that could not be misinterpreted. Liza realised with amazement and delight that even after marriage the ritual of courtship must always be renewed before each new onslaught.

So involved had they become, one with another,

that their consciousness had shrunk, and included now only the table, with its little pool of light encircling the two of them. Suddenly their island became an isthmus, as a street band, of the type one sees so often in Rome, entered the restaurant and made its way in a straggling line towards the couple, picking out tourists with ease. The accordions were insistent and discordant. Liza looked up, annoyance on her face. But could it be? Was it possible after four years? Enrico! The monkey face was as ancient and nut-like as ever; the tiny body still supported the huge accordion, as by a miracle. On one occasion she and Jonny had spent a whole night with Enrico. They had ended up in a dirty little trattoria behind the Forum, with Enrico producing half-a-dozen conceited Italian boys as possible suitors for Liza, and lamenting the fact, with laudable insincerity, that he, alas, was too old.

'Enrico, Enrico, you remember me? Liza, Irlandesa?' Enrico had obviously no idea who she was, but he gallantly took off his hat, swept a bow and said, 'Of course ... of course, *bella, pui bella.*' He kissed her hand, and began to play, a sentimental Sicilian tune. Stephen ordered more wine, they sat together, they talked. For hours they talked, the ridiculous, extravagant Roman bonhomie, false and seductive, replacing the limitations of words.

As they strolled back to the hotel, Liza was a little unsteady on her feet. Stephen took her arm, guiding her. In the lobby she stopped. 'You go on up, Stephen, I'm going to phone Jonny.'

'Darling, are you crazy, it's one o'clock in the morning. They'll all be in bed.'

'No, I'm going to phone him, I must.'

'Really, Liza, this is absurd, come on now ...'

27

'Oh please, Stephen,' she appealed to him.

'Well alright,' he sighed, 'I'll wait for you here.'

'No,' her voice was sharp. 'Leave me alone. Go up to bed, I told you I'd be up afterwards.' She noticed that Stephen looked surprised and hurt. His back seemed somehow vulnerable as he walked towards the stairs.

It took an age to get through to Dublin. The hotel porter who was helping her and the Roman operator seemed to chatter endlessly, laughing and joking. But Liza did not mind. She sat and savoured the Roman night. She remembered. How delighted Jonny would be that she had met Enrico again. The Dublin operator sounded cheerful. And finally she heard her own phone ring. It rang for a long time.

'I'm sorry, Rome, no reply.'

'Keep trying, please, just for another while.'

It rang out again, and then a cross voice said, 'Yes, who is it?'

She didn't wait for the Dublin operator. 'Jonny, it's me, Liza.'

'Liza, my God, what's wrong? Are you alright? Has something happened to Stephen?' His voice was no longer sleepy, but anxious as he fired the quick succession of questions.

'Don't be silly, Jonny, everything's fine. I'm in Rome. Rome, Jonny. And guess who I met tonight? Enrico?'

'Enrico who? For God's sake, Liza, shut up and stop wasting time. What *is* the matter?'

'I told you, nothing. I just wanted to ring to tell you that I met Enrico tonight. You remember the man who played the accordion in that restaurant, Mario's. I thought you'd be interested. You know . . .'

28

'Good God, Liza, have you gone mad? Ringing me at this hour of the night about nothing. Where's Stephen?'

'Upstairs waiting for me in our room.'

'Well, go to bed yourself, for goodness sake. Do you hear me, Liza?' His voice was stern and uninterested.

'Yes, Jonny. *Buona sera*.'

Quietly she put down the phone.

'*Grazie*,' she said to the night porter, gave him the money and sat once more in the lobby.

She sat and thought. She sat for a long time. A calmness settled on her as she examined her position. So she wasn't nineteen any more and her jeans didn't fit. She felt sad, but it was a pleasant nostalgic sadness. Life, she supposed, would be lived as a woman from now on. Perhaps it had always been so. It was hard to say. But one had certain consolations, had achieved certain realisations. For a short time, she had been mistress of her flesh. For a short time, she had come into her own. Once when she was nineteen and a virgin in Rome. With a brother and no money and tight blue jeans.

Hey Nonny No

Lucy, as usual, had arrived far too early. She knew that it took about half-an-hour to get to the airport, even in heavy traffic, and yet always she would panic and begin to imagine all the things that could go wrong and she would set out far too early, and sit as she was sitting now, twiddling her thumbs, drinking gin and waiting for the plane to arrive.

She fingered her new beret, yellow, pulled low down on her forehead, hiding all her hair, making it practically impossible to tell where golden hair ended and yellow beret began. She had bought it to go with her brown raincoat; to be truthful, she bought it also for Richard. But now she began to wonder if he would recognise her in it. They had only met twice before, on the first occasion very briefly, and both times she had got the impression that Richard had not seen very much. He had been dazzled — by the fact that she was Arthur's girl-friend?

Lucy wanted to feel wicked, and the gin was beginning to help. It would make a nice change feeling wicked, better certainly than feeling continually bruised. Well, that was over, Richard was the antidote for that. Tentatively she reached out a hand towards her jaw, her rib-cage, to feel if she still ached. She had carried round that ache, that all-enveloping ache, for two years. For two years she had walked in Arthur's shadow, smiling in his smile, darkening in his frown. She had sat on the edge of chairs, on the edge of bar-stools, anticipating his evolving thoughts, interpreting his slightest change in expression. Oh she had loved him right enough, and believing in the invincibility of her passion, she had thought herself loved in return. She had ignored the impatience, the sulking, the sudden unexplained disappearances. In fact she would be still ignoring them now if poor old Richard hadn't blundered in.

She and Arthur had been making love when the phone rang next door, and Arthur had heaved himself out of bed, saying that it might be important. He was one of those people to whom important things were always about to happen. He came back five minutes later, looking bad-tempered, and hurriedly began to put on his clothes.

'What's wrong?' she had asked.

'Oh nothing — just an idiot friend of my brother's who's over here on business. He's just rung up asking if he can come round. At this hour, for God's sake.'

'Why didn't you just say no, that you were busy?'

'Oh well, old Richard's not such a bad chap. A bit of an ass, awful old woman, but decent enough. And he has this foul marriage — ghastly female who nags him all the time. They never should have got married in the first place of course, they were never suited. That's why you and I are so much better off as we are. Anyway, as I said, he's a great buddy of Stephen's and Steve gave him my address to call when he came to Dublin. I haven't seen him — why, it must be five years now.'

The remark had been so casually slipped in that Lucy wondered if it could have meant anything

31

really.

'What do you mean?' she now asked.

'What?'

'What you said just now. That we were better off as we were. What is that supposed to mean?'

'Honey, you know, like this — as we are.'

'No, I want to know now. Do you mean never get married?'

'Jesus, women are all the same. The only thing they ever seem to think of is marriage. I don't . . .'

'I just want to know — what did you mean?'

Arthur walked over and sat on the side of the bed. He took her hand in one of his, and with the other smoothed back her dishevelled hair.

'Darling,' he said, 'I think you're a great girl. You're fun and you're generous and you're very clever. Far cleverer than me. But marriage — well, can you imagine us?'

'I don't see why not, if you've nothing against marriage as such.'

'Look, as I said, you're marvellous and we get along very well. But marriage, well, you need something more for that. Love for example. Now we don't love each other, and—'

'I love you, you bastard.'

'Please Lucy, don't get hysterical.'

She had burst into tears. Those suspicions deep in the subconscious had been well founded. But though Arthur patted her and kissed her, and kept telling her how marvellous she was, the obvious relief of at last having come out with the truth gave him the necessary courage to stand his ground. He did not love her.

She was still snivelling in the bed when the door bell rang. She couldn't stay shivering in there, she couldn't rush past Richard on the doorstep. Social convention came to the rescue. She would have to get dressed and then join the two of them for a civilised drink in the drawing room. Arthur shoved her into the bathroom, thrust her handbag at her and told her to go and do something with her face while he went to let Richard in.

When she reappeared, Arthur stood preening on the hearthrug — 'Darling, I'd like you to meet my very good friend, Richard Woods, over from London for a few days,' — and it was clear that he would not take it at all amiss if Richard should happen to gather that the rosy maiden standing in front of him was flushed and limp-looking from satisfactory bedding.

From that first moment Lucy felt a sympathy for Richard. 'We're two of a kind,' she thought, as she watched him cackling wildly at Arthur's sallies and blundering on through inane conversations. 'We will always be put at a disadvantage by the Arthurs of this world.' He was a small, rotund man, with a pink-and-white face and blond curls. He had probably been an angelic child, but at forty he looked faintly ridiculous. He wore a well-cut tweed suit and highly polished brown brogues. But the end product was too painstaking. Arthur, beside him, looked insolently and casually elegant.

'He's going down to Cork tomorrow, but he wants us to have dinner with him on Thursday when he gets back. Both of us.' Arthur had just seen Richard to his taxi — he had stayed only half-an-hour. 'I don't think I can face it though. Christ — he's an even bigger bore than I remember.'

Arthur was talking now as if nothing had passed between him and Lucy. His casual good humour was the same as it always had been, but if *he* had been given strength earlier, Lucy was feeling it

33

now. This, she was determined, was the end. Her tears were shed, a scab was already beginning to form over the wound. Her anger suddenly blazed out at Arthur. '*You* needn't meet him, I don't see why you should when you have such obvious contempt for him. But I will, I'll have dinner with him on Thursday. I'd be delighted.'

Arthur refilled her glass. 'Rather you than me. But watch out that he doesn't begin to play on your maternal instinct. That's how Jane was trapped, they say.'

He smiled and Lucy supposed that it was a measure of his indifference to both of them that even in the circumstances he didn't see their meeting as a threat to his position.

The following Thursday Lucy was waiting in the hotel bar when Richard came down. He was wearing a dark suit and his curls had been brushed into submission. He began to fuss right away — was the drink all right, had he kept her waiting, was she warm enough?

'I'm sorry Arthur couldn't make it,' he said, 'but I'm glad you came along anyway. I hope it's not presumptuous of me to say that I was looking forward to meeting you again.'

'It's not presumptuous of you at all, not if you mean because I'm Arthur's girlfriend. There's nothing between us, you know, we've just known one another for ages. Purely platonic relationship.'

He looked confused, glanced away, took a quick sip of his drink and then smiled shyly at her. 'Oh, I thought, well, that is I assumed that it was — well, serious.'

'Absolutely wrong. We'd hardly be very suitable for one another — would we?'

'Actually,' he rushed in eagerly, 'I thought that the other night. I hope you don't mind me saying so, Arthur's a very fine chap, but he had a bit of a reputation with the ladies in London. And you seemed so — untinselly, not flashy enough for Arthur's world. Too beautiful in fact.' And he blushed and apologised and insisted on her having another drink. Lucy felt a rush of warmth for him. But as the night progressed and he talked on about his childhood and schooldays, she realized that what she was feeling was not warmth, but the cold wash of pity. Poor Richard, so intelligent, so sensitive, so irredeemably outside the club. In fact — she blushed shamefully — a bit of an old woman. His schooldays had been miserable. He had always hated games, had been bad at them and had suffered because of this and because of his size. He had been nicknamed 'Dicky-bird' as a result of his sissyness and his liking for poetry. Even after twenty years, the memory of those days was still painful. His father, an army man, had shared his schoolmates' opinion, and when he had died three years ago Richard realised that he had died still disapproving of his son. 'I was an only son, you see, and he had hoped I'd follow him into the army. But I couldn't, it would have been the same as school all over again. I must have been a great disappointment to him.'

At three o'clock that morning, as they sat in her car outside the hotel, she asked him about his wife.

'Jane? Well, she's a remarkable woman in many ways. And I've three children. Here, I'll show you their photographs. Do you want to see them?' He pulled out some black and white prints, somewhat the worse for wear. 'That's Anne, she's seven, and Gillian six, and Peter, he's four.' Lucy

35

looked at the solemn, dark-haired children — there seemed to be nothing of Richard in them.

'Have you any of Jane?'

'Actually, no, not with me that is.'

'Tell me a bit about her — what's she like?'

'Well, as I said, she's an excellent woman. A very good mother and very capable. I suppose that's why I irritate her so much.' He stopped and looked into the darkness.

'Yes?' Lucy prompted.

'I get on her nerves. I suppose we should never have got married. You see, she's two years older than me, she was at school with my sister. Everyone thought we should get married, that it would be a good idea. Oh, I did too — I admired Jane tremendously, she was always so handsome and sure of herself. But I'm not the right sort of husband for her.'

'Why not?'

'I suppose I'm too ineffectual, I'm not decisive enough. And I'm hopeless round the house and no good at parties. I think I began by irritating her, but now she despises me.'

'Poor Richard. She sounds awful.'

'No, no, she's not. It's just as I said, we're not suited. She should have married someone like my father.'

'Well, at least you have the children.'

'We do and they're marvellous kids. But that went wrong too. Jane won't any more — you know, she won't — not after Peter, she had a bad time then. And she won't go on the pill or let me use anything . . .'

He broke off and looked out the window. Even in the darkness, Lucy could see the misery flood into his face. She reached over and gently placed her hand on top of his, and they sat like that for some time, silently, and with a bond of sympathy and understanding growing between them. The wounded consoling the wounded.

An hour later, as Lucy was going to bed, she realised that she hadn't thought of Arthur once in the whole evening.

She called next day to say goodbye to Richard. She wanted to make him feel a little better, to show him some kindness. 'Take my address and phone number,' she said. 'You can give me a ring or write to me the next time you're coming over.' But he had done more than that. In the five weeks since their meeting he had written six letters, and she had replied. It had given her something to do.

Now she left the bar and went to the Arrivals area. The flight was in, she saw, although the passengers had not yet begun to come through. She hoped he wouldn't be last off; people she went to meet at airports always seemed to manage to be. And what about the beret, should she take it off? Then, she felt someone press her arm, and there he was standing before her, looking a little uncertain. She smiled and he took her hand and kissed her cheek. 'Let's have a drink.' She had difficulty hearing what he said, his voice was so low.

Back in the bar she sat down at the table she had vacated a few minutes before. The barman looked at her, and then looked away, indifferent. Richard had disappeared, gone to the lavatory she supposed. He reappeared with a gin-and-tonic for her and a whiskey for himself. It was as if no time had elapsed since their last meeting, now that the formalities were over.

'I've brought you a present,' he said.

'Oh?'

'Yes, a record. Open it.'

She took off the pink wrapping paper. ' "Songs from Shakespeare's Plays".' She turned over the back. ' "It Was a Lover and His Lass". "Mistress Mine, Where are You Roving?" '

'Youth's a stuff 'twill not endure,' sang Lucy and laughed at Richard. They both laughed. It was true, youth did not endure. She had spent too much time grieving over Arthur, and a man's a man for all that. She took Richard's hand and pressed it, and laughed again to discount the seriousness in his eyes.

'And how's Arthur?' he asked as they sat over their second drink.

'I don't know, I haven't seen him since.'

'Oh, I see.'

'Richard, listen, I have something to tell you about Arthur and myself. I wasn't frank about it the last time. You see, we *were* quite serious about it, about one another you know. We'd been going out together for about two years and Arthur wanted us to get married. I didn't know, I was never very sure, and then when you came over the last time, somehow you put things in perspective. I suppose I just realised, finally, that we weren't suited. It had nothing directly to do with you, it was just that you appeared to have so many of the qualities that he lacked. You crystallised things for me.'

Richard was looking at her with joy, but Lucy didn't notice. She was too busy marvelling at how one could state certain things which were absolutely true and still be so far from the truth.

'I'm hungry,' she said suddenly.

'Right — let's head for town then, shall we?'

'We can get the bus outside.'

'Certainly not, we'll get a taxi.'

'But Richard, you're ridiculous, it's miles into town and—'

'Special occasion. Taxi or nothing.'

All of a sudden Richard appeared very masterful as he swung her up, guided her outside and heaved her into a waiting taxi.

'Exchequer Hotel,' he said to the driver.

'Why are we going to your hotel?' Lucy found it difficult to get her tongue round the words. She had felt all right in the bar, but the gin had hit her as she came into the open air. 'Richard, are you going to seduce me, is that why you're taking me to your hotel?' She giggled at his face looming over her, shocked looking, the mouth agape.

'Lucy, of course not. I was going to leave my stuff there but if you'd prefer not to call we can—'

'Silly, I'm only joking. Anyway, I want you to seduce me, why don't you seduce me? Only,' she paused, and frowned in drunken concentration, 'if I want you to do it, then it's not seduction — is it?'

Richard didn't seem to notice the words, only their intention. He squeezed her hand. 'Lucy. Oh, Lucy.'

When the taxi drew up outside the hotel, Lucy awoke with a start, bumping her head against the window.

'I'm so sorry Richard, did I sleep all the way?'

'Yes, like a baby.'

'Did I snore?'

'Very gently.'

'Oh, I *am* sorry.'

'Stop apologising and let me pay the man.'

They entered the hotel. Richard went to the desk to check in.

'Tea?' Richard enquired.

'Yes, lovely.'

In the Residents' Lounge they sat and smiled and drank their tea in silence. Fellow-conspirators.

'Are you sure you want to?'

'Don't be silly.'

'Right. Then I'll get the lift and you walk up. It's on the fourth floor, number forty two. I hope you don't mind, but they're fairly sticky here I imagine, and your reputation, you know.'

Like a thief she ran up the stairs, terrified, expecting to be challenged at any moment. She met a chambermaid and thought that she gave her an odd look. Then she was on the fourth floor and she could see Richard's head poking out half way down the corridor. She ran to meet him and he walked towards her, pulling her in and locking the door behind them. Laughing, they fell together on the bed.

Afterwards they lay together, sticky and hot. For minutes neither of them stirred. Lucy wished she could move away to a cooler part of the bed. But she was too limp. Richard was certainly a wonder. Finesse, that's what he possessed — not like that bastard, Arthur. But she could forget about *him* now, he was a thing of the past, he had been exorcised today. She would forget him, consign him to oblivion, start again herself. Pastures new, endless possibilities just around the corner. She sighed and could almost believe herself content.

Richard gazed lovingly at the back of her head, tousled on the pillow so near him, and reached out to touch her. She felt his touch and turned round. She smiled at him. Such a battered face, furrows of suffering and pain, and here and there the beginnings of decay. Lucy knew, without the assurance of the looking-glass, that her own face was smooth and flawless. It would take several more Arthurs and several more years before anything began to show. But poor Richard — next month, next year, two years' time, would she not be etching another ridge adown that jaw? She felt sad at the thought of the sufferings she would inflict on him. But it was an abstract sadness, a regret that the nature of man — and woman — should be thus. Unfortunate, but a fact of life. That's where moralists were wrong — suffering didn't ennoble, it merely hardened. Yes, poor old Richard, she would be sorry to see him go. She would almost miss him.

Compassion

As I look back over the years — some thirty years from young adulthood until now — I know one thing with certainty. I know that I have grown in compassion. It is pleasant to feel that there is some plus quantity in the midst of all the wreckage; and it is a feeling that many of my age-group may share. For although it is obviously true that some young people are tolerant and have pity to spare, I do not think, on the whole, that compassion comes naturally to the young. They are too preoccupied with their own griefs and problems to pause long enough to consider the condition of others. To-day, I always endeavour to look behind the facade, to seek out the wounded soul lurking there. And I usually find it. Is it the competitiveness of youth that makes it so eager to condemn?

Twenty-four years ago I was teaching in a large Dublin school. At least it was considered large in those days, and very modern and progressive. Perhaps it was in order to give some substance to this reputation for modernity that Mother de Lourdes, the mistress of schools, employed mainly a young lay staff. Certainly it was unusual, at that time, to find five women, all under thirty, employed in a Convent Secondary School.

I was somewhat older than the others — I was twenty-nine then — and I know that two of them

42

were straight from College, which would put them at no more than twenty-two. But despite the age difference, we were all very close. We became tremendous friends, spending a great deal of time in each other's company. Two of us were from Dublin, one from Cork, one from Limerick, and one, Peggy, a native Irish-speaker from the Donegal Gaeltacht.

Even at that time, the teaching profession had, for many years, been an acceptable escape-route for the deserving working class. The bright, hard-working small-farmer's or labourer's son, while he could never hope to become a doctor or an archi-tect, could always gain a foothold into the middle-classes by becoming a teacher. But this was, I think, less true for women teachers, and particularly University-trained women teachers, and we five in the Convent of Jesus Our Saviour appeared as middle-class as you could find. Our bourgeois aura encompassed us, and although to-day we might be considered a smug lot, this smugness, as with many middle-class people, arose from ignorance — lack of imagination rather than any real arrogance. My father was a lawyer; his father had been a comfort-able farmer from the Golden Vale. As a family we accepted financial ease and an educated background as we accepted the colour of our eyes or the green of the grass. The other four, I had always assumed, came from similar backgrounds. I knew that Joan did, for I had spent one summer in her Sunday's Well home, a tall gracious house, like mine full of heavy mahogany furniture, but with a magnificent view up the river Lee.

And I think there was a certain basis for my assumption, for despite the romantic notion that we Irish have of ourselves of making one leap from the peasant's cabin to the good job in the Civil Service, scores of Irish families have, like my own, been sending sons to Clongowes College for three generations. The interesting thing about this class is that it is totally nationalistic in outlook. Despite the best efforts of the Jesuits there are no Englishmen *manque* here, and I know that my family has always been conscious of its Irish identity, and proud of it. It may have been this outlook, present in all of us, which caused a certain insensitivity in our reaction to, and therefore treatment of, Peggy.

By the time she arrived in the school, Joan, Rita, Shiela and I had already coalesced into a sort of group, a coterie. Our friendship had taken on a formality, and with this an obligation, so that we were like members of a very exclusive club. But we were cultural snobs, and I think the first thing that struck any of us about Peggy was that she would lend a certain distinction to our group. We considered that we had become friends because we were civilised people in an uncivilised world. Accordingly, we set ourselves a fairly rigid code of behaviour. Our interests being intellectual we never permitted ourselves to read women's magazines or listen to popular music on the radio. We patronised the theatre extensively, and the cinema selectively. We never boasted of money or holidays or boy-friends. In fact, it was an unwritten rule that boy-friends were mentioned in the most oblique fashion, and we observed this rule faithfully, both out of consideration for any member of the group who might not have a boy-friend, and out of disdain for anything that might smell of one-upmanship. Our victories were always moral. At the time Peggy joined us I was enjoying a particular moral distinction, for I had just captured — temporarily, as it turned out — the most eligible bachelor in town. He was a young University don whose work in the field of literary criticism was making people in England and America sit up and take notice. He was never mentioned by me to one of the group except as 'a friend of mine,' and I would feel a glow of satisfaction as Joan would look at me, first appraisingly, and then with approval. It appeared to us that our subtleties knew no bounds.

Anyone reading this may see us as young prigs, but I think such a view would be unkind and unjust. There was nothing particularly wrong with our life style, and there was much that was admirable in our idealism — it was simply that we took ourselves and each other so seriously. Most young people do, and we were determined to leave our mark on life. We were also totally loyal to each other. In school we exchanged ideas, helped one another with work, covered up if one of us was late. Outside school we always spent Wednesday evenings and Sunday afternoons together, all five of us. We adhered strictly to this routine and none of us would dream of making a date for either of these days. Otherwise we kept our lives largely apart. I think now that the reason for this was that such austerity had to be tempered by a more relaxing style of living during the rest of the week.

Wednesday evenings were devoted to our cultural sorties, and after some time we achieved through them a certain acclaim. As a group we shared above average good looks, and we all believed in *la bella figura*, but on Wednesday evenings it had to be a corporate one. Thus, before we set out to a concert, or a theatre or a cinema we would plan carefully together what each one would wear. The group must look distinguished, the figures must blend; as in dressing a play, the total effect was what was important. Then we would 'appear together, the five of us, in the foyer of a cinema or theatre, smiling, slightly distant, absorbed in ourselves. Our conversations on such occasions had a formality too, and it was understood that they would be serious, carried on in measured tones, no idle chatter.

How we enjoyed discussing afterwards the sensation we had caused. Sometimes someone well-known would be discovered eyeing us with interest, and the speculation would become wild; we would undoubtedly appear in a poem, be the mysterious heroines of some play. The effect we had on men delighted us. We would note the admiring glances, and then the puzzlement. We felt as we thought film-stars must feel, and we all agreed that it was totally understandable that one man could never hope to satisfy such as they.

Sunday afternoons were spent either in my house or Rita's, we being the only two with homes in Dublin. I had a bedroom on the top floor of our house, looking out over the garden to the mountains beyond. I turned it into a bed-sittingroom, filling it with large silk cushions, swathing my electric light bulbs in downy pink, fixing adhesive round the door and windows to exclude draughts. Before the others arrived I'd light a log fire, and by four o'clock the room was scented, softly shadowed and warm. With a record playing mutedly on the gramophone, it was an oasis of comfort and security in the gloom of a winter afternoon. At five, Elsie would bring the tea.

It was all rather affected, but quite harmless. I'm sure I saw myself as a literary hostess and my bedsit as my salon. We were all afflicted with extreme self-consciousness so that even drinking a cup of tea became a ritual. But how we enjoyed ourselves at our tea-parties and our outings. Life has never held the same piquancy for me since, and anytime nowadays that I smell China tea, I am instantly transported back to those Sunday afternoons.

When Peggy had been a month or so in the school, we asked her to join us one week-end. She arrived at my house earlier than the others, and sat like a mouse all through the afternoon. She never lost this shyness, and even when she had known us for eight or nine months she still never proferred an opinion or suggested a particular play or film that we should see. We found this altogether charming, and she became the pet of the group, protected by the rest of us, indulged in her difference.

Later however, she began to assert herself in the most distressing manner. The second year, when she came back after the summer holidays, we noticed a change at once. She looked different for a start, brighter, harder, almost common. She immediately launched into an account of her marvellous holiday in Venice. We were prepared to forgive her — we suspected that it was the first time she had ever been abroad, and we approved of her choice. But then, for our first Wednesday outing, she turned up in a most outrageous dress, scarlet and shining and deeply décolleté. It was quite appalling, and none of us could understand it, for as usual we had planned our corporate ensemble, and had all decided on muted autumnal tones, particularly suitable for the first week in September. She looked at us brazenly as she walked into the theatre, sweeping back her head like a filly. It was a lapse, but we would accept it. It was perhaps natural that Peggy

47

might feel swamped by the rest of us and was now simply making an effort to assert herself. But we wished she had done it with more taste. The incident would have been forgotten if her continuing behaviour hadn't forced us to realise that something would have to be done.

Now, not satisfied with monopolising every conversation, she began to name-drop blatantly. She would tell us that she had had cocktails last week with Professor so-and-so, or that she had spent the previous evening discussing contemporary art with some well-known sculptor. We decided that Joan was the one to take her in hand. She was particularly kind and fine-grained, and could be trusted to point things out to Peggy without hurting her feelings. We never thought simply of dropping her; we were fond of her and she was one of us. Joan assured us that we need have no worries — she would do her best and we must continue to treat Peggy as if nothing were amiss.

She was as good as her word. Within three weeks we could see a change in Peggy's behaviour. She ceased to boast, and she began to dress more quietly again, more in harmony with the group. We were pleased. But our pleasure was to be short-lived, for soon Peggy was showing other, more disturbing, signs. She became very withdrawn, worse than when she had come to Dublin first. She never spoke at all unless we asked her something, and her former interest in our activities now turned to listlessness. But she still insisted on coming everywhere with us and doing everything that we did. Another meeting was obviously called for, and so one evening the rest of us sat down around my parents' dining table, believing that the seriousness of the occasion demanded something less frivolous than my bedroom.

At the end of three hours we decided that it was we who must have been at fault. Joan was convinced that she was particularly to blame. She felt that Peggy must have been offended by some comment she had made. She had tried to be careful, to think of every possible interpretation of everything she said, but now she felt that, obviously, she had not succeeded. The rest of us, however, could not agree with this. We were all responsible and we should have realised long ago how shy and timid Peggy was and let her continue in her absurd fashion if she had to. As the eldest of the group I felt a special responsibility, and I decided I'd take her under my wing from then on. I would bring her out more on her own, even encourage her to talk about her famous boy-friends. I was determined to make amends.

And I did. I took to walking home from school with her, and I'd ask her about her boy-friends, and tell her how pretty she was and how much I envied her her lovely hair. I took her out to see my aunt in Monkstown, where I hoped my cousin Larry, who was about her age, might become interested in her. That day was a disaster however, for Peggy was at her worst, spilling her sherry and staring round her like a terrified sheep. I wanted to shake her but I had to feel sorry for her too — she was obviously going through agonies. I took her out to tea and coffee, and indeed I was soon devoting the major portion of my leisure time to her.

But I didn't mind too much. I was still experiencing pangs of guilt, and felt that it was no more than just that I should be inconvenienced as punishment for my transgression. The others all helped of course, and gradually our patience began to pay off. Peggy became less withdrawn; she began to offer

49

opinions readily and altogether seemed to grow more relaxed in our company. And, although she lapsed occasionally, she seemed to be boasting less. One evening Joan suggested that it would be a good idea if we asked her to give us Irish lessons. It would be a boost to her ego, and she'd feel at last that *she* had something to teach *us*. Besides, it might be quite fun. Shiela agreed and said that as she'd forgotten her Irish, she'd welcome the opportunity of learning some again. Peggy seemed pleased enough, and so, from then on, on every second Sunday we had two hours of Irish conversation. Rita and Shiela, who had some acting ability, would often improvise a little play, Rita with a scarf round her head as a shawl acting out the part of the long-suffering wife, and Shiela, with a cap specially bought for the purpose, promising her that he would give up the drink. Or some such nonsense.

These antics had been going on for about five months — none of us learning much Irish but having tremendous fun — when one evening after school Mother de Lourdes summoned Joan and myself to her office. She handed us a brown envelope, dog-eared and with her name scrawled on it. 'Open it,' she said, 'and read it.' Inside, written in clumsy block capitals on a piece of cheap lined note-paper, were the words: 'Do you know what kind of women you are employing? Ask them what corruption they get up to at their get-togethers.' Naturally, it was unsigned.

We were so shocked that neither of us could say anything for some moments, and then we both broke out together, crying inarticulately of our disgust, our revulsion at such obscenity. Mother de Lourdes took us both by the hand and tried to calm us. 'I know, my dears, I know how you must feel. It is quite appalling, but you had to know. I couldn't rest tonight with that . . . thing lying on my desk. Now that I've told you, I am going to burn it and forget about it and say a prayer for whoever perpetrated such a deed. They need prayer. Let us all try to forget about it.'

But we were not allowed to do so. Next morning Mother de Lourdes received another note and the morning after that, another. The letters were always shoved under the convent door, presumably at night — the wall at the end of the drive was low and easy to get across even when the gates were locked at ten. Over and over again we asked ourselves who could have sent them. Who could hate us enough to want to? The insinuations were vague in all three letters, but in a sense this made them worse, for the hints of decadence and evil were more upsetting than a specific accusation. We were all girls who had been surrounded with love and admiration all our lives and what stunned us most was the venom of the writer.

Then the sixth day of that terrible week, Joan came to me before class, white-faced and trembling. She drew me aside and handed me the now familiar bit of paper. I took it and spread it out.

'You think you have a nice cushy set-up you and your friend Anne Tierney but the joke's on you. Her father fucks her every night. Ask her how she likes it.'

Of course, we couldn't show this to Mother de Lourdes — it was too horrifying for anyone else to see — but equally we could not let it go any further. God knows what might happen if this continued. We decided on a plan which we would carry out ourselves. The letters to the convent were

51

delivered by hand, presumably sometime after the nuns had gone to bed. All Joan and I had to do was lie in wait behind the rhododendron bushes near the front door. We would stay there till dawn if necessary.

The first night we took up our positions, armed with flasks of coffee and woollen rugs. We arrived at nine-thirty and were well dug in by the time Dan the handyman went down to lock the gates. At half-past ten we saw the lights go out one by one in the nuns' cells. Our vigil was long and cold and fruitless. By the time dawn was breaking, we were frozen and sleepy, and not a thing had passed by the driveway, not even a stray cat. Saturday night followed the same pattern and on Sunday we were prepared for another sleepless vigil and were both dreading the thought of a full day's school next morning. By twelve o'clock Joan was nodding off beside me but I was too cold and too cramped to be able even to rest in comfort. As I drew the rug closer around me, suddenly I heard, from the direction of the gate, the scuffing of gravel. It was a still night and the footsteps that now started up the driveway were magnified in the silence. I nudged Joan awake, and we sat there, clutching one another, shaking with terror. The footsteps approached inexorably, and then Peggy stepped out in front of us into a shaft of moonlight. I could see her profile and the fair sheen of her hair. She was wearing the plaid coat that she always wore to school. We both started forward. 'Peggy,' we gasped involuntarily. She turned quickly in the direction of our voices, and recognising us even in the shadows, wheeled abruptly round and broke into a run. As she ran, something fell from her hand. We knew what it would be before we went to retrieve it. There was no need to open the brown envelope.

We never mentioned Peggy again. Next day we told everything to Mother de Lourdes, and within hours there was a vacancy for an Irish teacher in the convent of Jesus Our Saviour. We had to tell Rita and Shiela also, but once we had done so the matter was closed. Shortly afterwards, the group began to break up. We did have one tea-party in my bed-sitting room but it was not a success. We were all painfully embarrassed and glad when it was time to go. That July I applied for a post in Wicklow.

Two years later I had bought a new car and was visiting an aunt of mine in Sligo. When I was there I suddenly realised how near I was to Donegal, and on impulse I decided to drive up. I had no definite plan, but after a day's driving I found myself in Peggy's townland. I had no fear of meeting Peggy, for I had heard indirectly that she was still in the local mental hospital where she had been sent after her breakdown on leaving Dublin. I knew she had a sister called Annie whom she had often talked about, and I stopped at the post-office and asked the post-mistress for directions to Annie McMenamin's house.

The road that I took was full of pot-holes and twisted through bleak and barren bog. After about two miles it began to peter out, and I thought I had been misdirected, when I saw on my right, sheltered by a few deformed trees, a low white-washed cottage. It was little bigger than our tool-shed at home, and not as well built. The front walls had been discoloured by cow-dung and the tiny windows were curtainless. In front of the door, a few hens pecked dispiritedly in the mud. Suddenly the door opened and a man appeared. He was wearing a collarless shirt and his trousers were held up with twine. He was carrying an enamel basin and he emptied its contents over a stunted hedge. Then he paused, cleared his nose between finger and thumb, and this too went over the hedge. The door was slammed shut again and the hens continued to peck.

I looked at Peggy's home, and I remembered with a painful sharpness all those Sunday afternoons of two years ago. I remembered Peggy McMenamin and the disintegration of our dreams. And do you know what I felt as I looked at the desolate scene? I felt resentment. Not pity, not understanding — much less compassion. Nothing but resentment.

The Birthday Girl

Mrs. Browning, a happily married mother of four, turned over the square of coloured card and smiled ruefully. Inside Stella had written: 'Happy birthday, Mum. Lots of love from all of us.' Mrs. Browning knew that later that day Stella would ring up her father to remind him and he would return home bearing a bottle of medium sherry and a bunch of roses; and pretending he hadn't really forgotten, he would kiss his wife's cheek and say playfully — 'And where would the birthday girl like to have dinner tonight — eh?' It was the same every year, and although every year Stella reminded them and reminded them, hers was the only card that ever arrived in the morning post. Mrs. Browning didn't mind, good heavens, of course she didn't, she wasn't that foolish. She knew perfectly well that remembering dates was just something that some people were good at, and besides, she had never been one to fuss over such frills. Stella was a darling, but then so were the other children, so was Leo. They were all simply different, and she realised this and had accepted it years ago. No, that wasn't what was making her feel dejected, she had felt awful from the moment she had woken up. Fifty years of age — half a century; well, that was enough to depress anyone.

Slowly, almost feebly, Mrs. Browning stood up,

and turning her back on the kitchen she began to walk upstairs. Her footsteps on the polished boards filled the empty house with a noise that echoed inside her head. She opened her bedroom door. The room was bathed in sunshine and although the window was open, a warm, fleshy smell still hung in the air. She sat down on the unmade bed and looked around her. For twenty-three years she had woken up in this room; for twenty-three years she had lain in this bed. She remembered the day she had moved in as a bride, the wall-paper had been pink then. Her mother, standing where she was sitting now, had turned and said, 'Well, Harriet, you won't be like me, starting off in two rooms. You're one of the lucky ones. Why, this is the sort of house one could happily spend a lifetime in.' Three of the children had been born in this bed — she had refused to go to a nursing-home after Sean. The wall-paper had been changed three times, she remembered, and the carpet twice. Mrs. Browning, suddenly filled with despair, got up and started walking around the sun-drenched room. 'But what more?' she kept on asking herself. 'What more?' It was a senseless question, she didn't even know what she meant by it, any more than she knew why a feeling of panic was gripping her stomach. She had a good husband and a lovely family and a delightful house; it was the thirty-first of July and the sun was shining, and dear Jesus, if she didn't get out, get away, escape, she would, she really would lose her mind.

She steadied her shaking hands against the edge of the mattress and tried to get hold of herself. It was simply that she wasn't getting out enough, she was too much cooped up in the house on her own. She mustn't give in to herself, no use being silly.

What was she afraid of anyway? But even as she reasoned with herself, a wave of panic overtook her again. She could not stay here for another minute.

At the bus-stop at the end of the road, a handsome, middle-aged woman stood waiting. She appeared cool and self-possessed, except if you looked very closely you might notice a strain around the eyes. But that in itself was no more than might be seen on many faces. Mrs. Browning *was* feeling better. She thought, with a sort of relish, of the unmade beds and the unwashed crockery. It was not that she minded doing housework — she never had particularly — but the fact that she had left her morning chores unfinished seemed to her a symbol of her breaking out. She was getting away from —? Well, when she came to think of it, she didn't really know, unless it was from herself. But she *was* getting away.

The bus came trundling round the corner like a brightly painted elephant and Mrs. Browning decided to sit upstairs so that she could really view the world. Besides, it emphasized the difference in the morning. Normally she would be one of those bleak-faced matrons who filled the lower deck at this time, leaving their outer suburb to drink coffee in town or have their hair done, or maybe seek out an adventure. The upper deck was empty apart from Mrs. Browning and one young man who sat two seats in front of her. His head was slightly inclined and she noticed the tender wisps of hair that lay silkily on his shirt collar. She could imagine how soft they felt. She snatched back her hand in the act of reaching out to stroke. Mrs. Browning's chest expanded with a flood of hope. What pleasure

57

she got from looking at that young man's neck; how many years, how many centuries since she had felt like that, a lightening of the spirit, a quickening of the flesh. Pleasure was a quality which had been receding from her life, imperceptibly, as youth had receded, as life itself would eventually recede. Well, she hadn't turned her back on it yet.

Standing on the city street where the bus had deposited her, she blinked at the sky. So much light, she was dazzled. People, dozens of people, hurried past purposefully, not even throwing her a curious glance. People with something to do. But what am *I* to do, she thought, now that I'm here. She moved forward a few steps and caught a glimpse of a figure, something familiar about it, in a shop mirror. 'Why it's me.' She stopped in amazement. 'That stoutish, frightened-looking woman is me.' Covertly she studied her image, slyly noting the good bag and shoes, the discreet dress, the overall dullness. So that was what people saw when they looked at her. A worn-out, used-up woman, almost ready for the scrapheap. But I am untouched, I am a girl as far as living is concerned, protested Mrs. Browning. That cannot be me.

Repudiating the figure, she fled down the street and scurried for refuge into a large store that opened in front of her. The air was scented, she stood and gazed around. Oh, such magic, such an array of colours and silks. Shyly she looked at the gorgeous painted girls who posed, hands poised on hips, gliding languidly or swaying their bodies to the rhythm of the music that came from loud-speakers all over the shop. Mrs. Browning moved from counter to counter, timidly, when she was unobserved, smelling the pots of creams and lotions, feeling satin blouses, gossamer tweed dresses, real

58

silk scarves. The beauty of it all, the extravagance, the wealth! Unsteadily she mounted the staircase, tipsy from such excess. An endless vista of dresses met her eye, rail upon rail, every length, every colour, every conceivable style. She wandered among them, sensuously letting her cheek brush against one, caressing another with the back of her hand. Then she saw it, a real beauty, tucked away at the end of a rack. It was pearl grey, and the material, oh the material! She whipped it off the rail and ran towards a dressing room, barely acknowledging the assistant who held the curtain back. Inside, she calmed herself, carefully putting down her bag, methodically undoing her fasteners and buttons. Then she took a deep breath, lifted the dress over her head and heard it rustle as it slid down her body. Fearfully she opened her eyes and looked in the glass. She gave a gasp of pleasure. The grey material clung to her body, moulding it into graceful lines, the colour just matched her eyes. Proudly her neck rose from the cunning folds, her hips seemed rounder and smoother, so elegant beneath the pleats of the skirt. She twirled round and the material rose and fell, luxurious and supple. Belatedly she looked at the price tag — sixty-five pounds. She had never spent that much money on one item of clothes, not even on a winter coat, but now it meant nothing to her. Calmly she drew out her cheque book — Leo and she had a joint account — and filled out the cheque without a single qualm. She knew she was probably spending the rates money, or money set aside for school expenses, but really, that was no concern of hers. She couldn't worry about such things, they had nothing to do with her any more. She undid the price tag and handed the cheque to the assistant.

'Are you wearing it, Madam? Shall I wrap your other dress?' Mrs. Browning looked with distaste at the crumpled garment. 'Oh, throw it away my dear, use it as a duster,' she said, laughing gaily.

Outside in the sunshine again she looked around her with new confidence. She sniffed at the world with sharpened senses and a growing feeling of excitement. 'I'm me,' she said, smiling to herself, 'I'm anonymous me, not Mrs. Browning any longer.' She did feel anonymous, invisible almost, and this anonymity was giving her a new security, a sensation that all sorts of things were suddenly within her compass. She paused before a cinema, her attention caught by the picture of a beautiful woman displayed on the bill-board. The show was just starting, it would be interesting to find out more about that woman, Liv Ullman she saw her name was. She bought her ticket, a pullman seat, and then at the kiosk, a box of Black Magic. Inside, it was half-deserted and Mrs. Browning chose a seat in the middle of a row some way down the aisle. She popped a chocolate in her mouth and with a sigh stretched out her legs; she had never before been to the cinema on her own and only half-a-dozen times in the afternoon, but after about ten minutes she began to think that something was wrong. The beautiful woman on the screen was having problems also. She sat unhappily in some house in some suburb of Stockholm and worried and fretted. What she was fretting about was no clearer to Mrs. Browning than were her own problems, but despite this lack of knowledge, she wanted to cry out, there, in the darkened cinema, 'No, it's all wrong. It's not like that at all.' There was too much glamour, too much glossiness, that woman's predicament seemed bearable, almost desirable. 'It's

60

untrue,' whispered Mrs. Browning, 'it's much worse than that, there isn't enough — terror.'

Abruptly she stood up and groped her way towards the exit, stumbling over the outstretched legs of a man snoring in an outside seat. In the foyer she paused to gather herself together, and glancing down at her dress, rubbed her hand over its silkiness for reassurance. It had been a foolish impulse to go and bury herself in a cinema on such a lovely afternoon. There was still some warmth in the sun, even though its rays had begun to shorten. She retraced her steps, back over the bridge, and catching a whiff of frying onions from some hamburger café, remembered that she had had no lunch. The realisation cheered her up. She must be getting away from herself; she hadn't forgotten lunch or any meal for the last twenty years, not once. Well, she wasn't going to have it now, just because she had remembered it, she would have a drink instead. In fact, several drinks. She'd go to one of the big city hotels, she liked their air of leisured opulence, the pampered feeling they engendered in one. She'd have a gay old time.

At the glass door marked 'Cocktails' she hesitated, and then smoothing her skirt and straightening her shoulders, walked boldly in. It was very dark inside, difficult to see, but finding an unoccupied chair in an inconspicuous corner, she slid into it. Timidly, she looked around, her eyes growing accustomed to the gloom. Apart from a man sitting at the bar, she seemed to be the only customer. It must be in-between times, she decided. She put her bag on the table and sat and waited. But the barman either hadn't seen her or was ignoring her. She coughed and then was horrified at how loudly it sounded in

61

the quiet room. Still neither the man on the high stool nor the barman paid any attention. She looked around for a bell, but there didn't seem to be one. She moved her chair forward, then stood up and raised her arm for attention, but the barman stood resolutely polishing his glasses, staring into space. Helplessly, Mrs. Browning sat down. What was she to do now? She was humiliated by the suspicion that she was being deliberately ignored, and all she wanted to do was slink out the door unnoticed. But, 'No, I won't,' she addressed herself sternly. 'I want a drink, why should I let them frighten me away.' Before she could change her mind she marched up to the bar. If he still ignored her, she would just say, 'Excuse me, please, I'm waiting to be served.' But she needn't have worried, for as she approached he was already putting down his cloth. The other man too turned to her. 'Why hello,' he said, 'another lost soul. I was beginning to think I was the only drinker left in the whole of Dublin. It was beginning to get lonely.' She could see from the carefully focused eyes that he was not quite sober, although his voice was clear and his words unblurred. She looked at him with sympathy. Last week she might have dismissed him, turned away, but today she had learnt too much to condemn a man for getting drunk. Deliberately she gave him a friendly smile. At first he seemed surprised, but then he smiled back. Poor fellow, he had obviously expected to be frozen out.

'Won't you join me, my dear?'

The 'My dear' sounded respectful, he was a few years older than Leo.

'Thank you, yes, I will.'

The barman gave her a look, but she didn't care. She was regaining that marvellous sense of freedom.

62

'Good, great,' the man said, rubbing his hands together. 'By the way, my name is Harry, and I have the honour of addressing —?'

'Liv,' she answered idiotically.

'Eh? Come again?'

'Liv.'

'Yes, well, live and let live I always say. And what will you have to drink, Liv?'

She looked at the alarming display of bottles. 'Oh, I'll have whatever you're having.'

'Two more Bloody Marys then, Gerry, there's a good lad,' Harry said, and turning, gave her a rather painful dig in the ribs. 'Live dangerously — what?'

Like a seasoned toper, Mrs. Browning knocked back her Bloody Mary. She had always been fond of tomato juice.

'This is my round,' she said, opening her bag.

'Hey, steady on. It's not etiquette to outstrip the master, you know.'

'Well, hurry up then. Live dangerously, as you said yourself.'

How good she was at it, you'd think to listen to her that she made a habit of picking up strange men. She had had no idea it would be so easy.

The next round arrived and they clinked glasses and smiled at each other. The bar was beginning to fill up and Harry moved his stool nearer to her, protectively, she thought.

'Well, Liv,' — as he leaned across her she could see the pores like craters in his well-shaped nose — 'Well now, I certainly never thought when I came out for a lonely drink that I'd end up in such charming company. This was a bit of luck for me. Makes a change I can tell you, having a pretty lady sitting beside you.'

It was a bit of luck for her too, if he only knew.

She had forgotten that flirtation could be so delicious. And he was so correct at the same time, not over familiar, never making her feel cheap. It just showed, sober or drunk, breeding counted. He was very well-spoken, she noticed, had a lovely rich voice.

Another drink had been deftly placed in front of her. As she went to fumble for her purse, a hand was gently placed over hers.

'My dear,' the pressure on the hand was increased, 'my dear, I do wish you'd realize it is an honour for me to be allowed to buy you a drink.'

'Yes, but I'm sure —'

'No buts. As I said, it isn't often I have such good fortune. I am essentially, Liv, a lonely soul, isolated you might say —'

'Isn't that extraordinary, I was just feeling the same way —'

'Yes, a lonely soul and one who therefore appreciates all the more such a fruitful, if fortuitous meeting.'

He paused grandiloquently and studied the liquid in his glass.

'Excuse me, Harry, I hope you don't mind my asking or think I'm being personal or anything, but, I was just wondering, you have such a distinguished way of speaking, are you by any chance — that is, do you act?'

His laugh was resonant. 'Why, constantly, dear lady, my whole life you could say —'

'No, but you know what I mean, is it your profession like?'

'Alas, dear lady, nothing so colourful. You are looking now at a much duller bird I fear — the humble lawyer.'

'Oh, not at all,' she hastened to reassure him. 'I

don't think there is anything dull about being a lawyer! In fact you could say that the two professions have a lot in common. I mean —' But as she spoke she was suddenly overcome by a wave of nausea. The bottles in front of her had begun to rotate in winking circles. Oh no, she couldn't get sick here. Why had she drunk so much? 'Excuse me, please,' she said between closed teeth and, carefully sliding off her stool, she began to navigate her route to the Ladies.

Her face in the mirror horrified her, cheeks deadly pale, eyes and nose red, hair dishevelled. Going into one of the toilets, she locked the door and sat down on the floor with her head between her knees. Soon she began to feel better and gritting her teeth she determined she would stay like that; keep off alcohol, that was the way. Having tidied up she returned to the bar, only to see at once that Harry had bought her another vodka. Well, perhaps if she drank it very slowly it would have no ill effects. She took a cautious sip, it was delightfully cool.

'Feeling alright, my dear? You looked a bit pale just now.'

'Thank you, I'm fine, I just thought it was very hot suddenly, but I'm grand now.'

He smiled at her solicitously and Mrs. Browning took another, less cautious swallow. She was really feeling very well again. She remembered reading somewhere that many illnesses were just imaginary, Freudian, because of some guilt the person was experiencing. She must have been feeling guilty about enjoying herself with an attractive man, that was all it was. Right, that could be settled easily enough.

'D'you know, Harry, I think I'd like a cigarette.'

'My dear, I *am* sorry, I thought you said —'

'Oh, I did, I don't normally smoke, it's just that I feel like one suddenly, if you don't mind.'

'Pleasure, make a night of it — what?'

She threw back her head, thinking of the grace of her throat in her lovely dress, and inhaled deeply. But as she did, before the smoke had even reached her stomach, she knew she had made a mistake. The nausea struck at her again, worse now. There was no time to excuse herself. She stood up, then stumbled against the stool, and fell sprawling on the broad of her back. The bar grew suddenly very silent and in the silence she heard Harry's voice, 'Jesus, she *is* drunk. This is all I need.' The blood flooded underneath her skin. She tried to get up, but couldn't. She could see her legs, like two white slugs exposed to the bar, her dress rucked up around her thighs, her shameful blue interlock knickers on display.

'Come on now, my dear.' Harry was trying to sound cool but his embarrassment was plain. 'Come on, I think it's time we got you a taxi.'

She allowed herself to be helped to her feet. People turned away as she stood up, deliberately engrossing themselves once more in their conversations. Harry's hand was in the small of her back, propelling her towards the door. She could feel the distaste in the pressure of that hand. She realized that she could have been sick in there for all she knew.

The porter gave them a knowing look. Harry handed him a note. 'Get her a taxi, will you,' he said, 'there's a good chap. I'm in a desperate hurry.' And he scurried out the door without a backward glance.

'And where shall I say you want to go, Madam?'

66

Mrs. Browning remembered that shining house. 'No, I don't want — I've no address. Leave me alone.' She collapsed onto a bench and sat there, sprawled and sobbing.

'I'm sorry, Madam, but you can't stay here.'

'Go away, go away, for pity's sake — leave me alone,' she bawled. Guests passing in and out were looking at her askance. The porter, visibly flustered, stood over her.

'Look here, do you want a taxi or will I call the police? There's a squad car just outside.'

The police! She couldn't allow that to happen. She pictured herself arriving home in a squad car, the neighbours looking out, the shame of Leo and the children. Opening her bag, she dragged out what money she had — two pound notes — and stuffed it into the porter's hand.

'I'm going home straight away, I was just being silly. But look, I must just go to the Ladies and tidy up a bit. My husband, you know — you can order the taxi for me.'

Like a mouse, she sat in the back of the battered Mercedes and looked out the window. Impossible to believe that it was only about six hours since she had left home. The dull weight of her misery numbed her and she sat, unseeing, as the car sped through the early evening streets. It was not until they were almost there and the driver turned round to ask which side that she suddenly saw the house, gleaming amidst its smooth lawns.

'That's it,' she said to the taxi man, and then she put down her head and hid her eyes in her sleeve. Mrs. Browning could not bear to look.

A Family Picnic

Mary Johnson opened her eyes to a room filled with yellow sunshine. Although the curtains were drawn, they hardly affected the light, for they were made of such thin stuff. In fact, they were not made of curtain material at all but of some summer dress material that her mother had bought at a sale in Clerys years ago when Mary was very small. They had been very carefully lined, however, and so hung properly. If Mary wished to get out of bed and walk across the still cold linoleum, she would see her mother's careful hand-stitching all around the inside of the curtains. They had never been able to afford a machine, so curtains had to be made by hand, sheets mended; even when Mary and her brothers were children, dresses and shirts had been hand sewn.

Mary stretched and yawned. Then she jumped out of bed, rushed over to the window and tore the curtains apart. The room was transfused with a strange luminosity. It was no longer her room with its shabby familiarity. It had become an abstraction in brightness and warmth. She stretched once more and, picking up the ends of her nightdress, stood on her toes and danced round and around in the sun. She danced her way to the window and collapsed in front of it, resting her chin on the ledge. She looked out into the garden. A cat sat

68

licking itself, half in shade, half in sunlight. A white butterfly fluttered around a dog-daisy before coming to rest on its yellow middle. The cat looked at it for a moment and then, indifferently, went back to cleaning its whiskers.

'We're going on a picnic today,' sang Mary, 'a pic-nic, pic-nic, pic-nic.' The words died away and faded into the heat of the morning outside. It was all so incredibly still.

Down in the kitchen, her father sat, stolidly eating his egg. Her mother bustled around, polishing his shoes, drinking a cup of tea, distractedly trying to think of the million and one things that had to be done. You couldn't leave a house, not even for a day, without seeing to so many things first. Still, it was a nice day for their outing.

'Morning Ma, Morning Daddy.' Mary sat down beside her father. She poured herself a cup of tea but then jumped up again and leaned across to the window. 'Let's open it,' she said. 'Why don't you open it and let in all that sunshine. You're missing it.'

Her father grunted, but didn't move away as the sashless window banged open and warmth wafted into the little room. He continued to scrape at his egg-shell in silence.

'No, no egg, Ma. I couldn't. You know I never eat eggs when it's this hot. I'll tell you what — hard-boil it and we'll take it with us. Then it won't be wasted.'

Reluctantly her mother put the egg back into the saucepan and onto the gas stove.

'I wish you would, Mary. I wish you'd eat properly,' she said. 'People like you who do so much brain work, they need proper nourishment. You'll end up with a nervous break-down if you go

69

on like that. People do, you know, when they don't eat properly.'

'Now, mother, we've had all this out before. You know I'm perfectly capable of dealing with my job — it's not all that taxing. You just think because I'm the only woman there that I must be killed trying to keep up. Anyway, I'm on holidays as from to-day. No brain work for a fortnight.'

Her mother smiled at her. Indeed she *was* able to keep up. Brains to burn. Always had. And what a lovely girl she was. Her girl. Always happy. She had never caused her parents a day's worry in her life. Not like the other two. Not like them. But she mustn't think of them today. They were all going on a picnic and the sun was shining. And if she didn't hurry they'd be late.

"Hurry up, Daddy, and finish your breakfast,' she said, taking the tea-pot away. 'We'll have to be off soon.'

They bundled into the little car, squeezing parcels and shopping bags where they could. Mr. Johnson had to bend his head in the back, the roof was so low. 'God,' he said, 'these seats would skin you — they're scorching.' Mary laughed at him. 'Stop complaining, Daddy. Think of Ma and myself with no trousers to protect us.'

Her mother sat beside her, rigid and straight-backed. She didn't think she'd ever feel at home in a car. Maybe it was because they'd never had one themselves. But Mary was great with the lifts. She never let you walk anywhere.

The road seemed still asleep as they set out. Nothing moved in the sun. The little houses lay dusty and still. No one was about, except for a few children, and even they hung limply over railings. It was already too hot to play.

'Now, we're not going to the sea. I've decided against it.' Mary's voice was imperious. 'It will be horrible on a day like this. All the trippers will be out in force, and nothing but mothers, babies and transistors everywhere. It would ruin the day. But I know just the place and I won't tell you. I'll keep it as a surprise. You just won't believe it when we get there. It is absolutely beautiful — much better than a crowded beach. I can't wait to show you.'

Mary's mother looked a little wistful. She had been hoping that Mary would say they'd go to the sea. It was years since she'd been to the seaside. Not since Mary and the others were small. Then on a good Sunday she used to take them all off, with bottles of milk and sandwiches, and they'd spend the whole day on the beach. Mary used to love it in those days. How she used to enjoy paddling, screaming and running away from the big waves. And Daddy loved to have the house to himself. He'd go to bed with the papers. 'I'll have a bit of peace and quiet now,' he used to say. Still Mary was probably right. It would be very noisy and crowded today. She supposed it was because she herself so seldom went out, so seldom saw anybody except the family, that she liked a bit of noise and excitement. But Mary was right. And she was taking after her father in that respect.

They drove through the city streets. You could almost see the heat rising from the pavements. The odd messengerboy who passed looked as if he must fall off his bike, so slowly, slowly did he turn the pedals. People dragged their feet, knowing it was going to be another scorcher. Would this heatwave never end? As they crossed over O'Connell Bridge, the water of the river seemed to have completely dried up. All that remained was a sort of oozy

71

brown mud. They closed the car windows against the rancid smell of decay.

'Didn't I tell you,' said Mr. Johnson, from behind. 'This weather is unnatural. We were never meant to have heat like this in Ireland. Look at that river, and the smell of it.'

Mary looked in the driving mirror and shook her head at him. 'You're starting again, Daddy,' she said. 'You know perfectly well the Liffey always stinks to high heaven. We need more sunshine here, not less. People open up in the sun. We bloom — don't we, Ma? We're blooming at this very minute.'

They opened the windows again and sat back. Nobody said anything. It was too hot for talking. Besides, there was no need to talk: the happiness was palpable inside the little car. Mary's father forgot about the Liffey. Suddenly he could see them all, sitting there on their way to the picnic — blooming. They were like geraniums on the kitchen window-sill at home. The words Mary thought up — the ideas she got. Blooming.

Soon they were out in the country, travelling along a narrow road. There were tall thick hedges on each side, their tops far taller than the roof of the car. The light was coming to them as through a filter — a cool, green filter. How restful it was after the glare of the streets. Eye muscles could relax, eyes could open fully once again and gaze at all that greenery. Mary felt as if she could drink it. They could not see the countryside beyond the hedges; they were enclosed in a dark green tunnel that went on and coolly on. Occasionally the sunlight came through and dazzled them for a second. It was nice to be reminded that outside, just beyond the trees, the sun was blazing fiercely down.

'Now,' said Mary, 'you must both close your

eyes, and don't open them till the car stops. No cheating, Daddy. I've a great surprise for you.'

The car stopped and Mr. and Mrs. Johnson opened their eyes and the three of them looked out together. They had pulled up beside an iron gate. The gate was bolted, but beside it was a turnstile. And beyond the turnstile, stretching out in front of them, was a huge, green field. It lay there, amazingly even and flat, and intensely green. They had never seen a field as green before. It was like an enormous table-cloth spread out for them. There were splashes of yellow here and there where little clumps of buttercups grew. In one corner, resting in the shade of some oaks, three or four red cows lay, chewing lazily. And, right at the edge of the field, as if across an emerald piazza, the still soaring ruins of a Gothic monastery rose into the sky. Beyond the monastery, through one of the arched doorways, they could see something shining in the sunlight. Could it be — it must be — a river.

They started across the field, silent and in single file. Awe-struck, one or other of them stumbled occasionally as their eyes discovered some new wonder. They made their way through the ruined cloisters, the gravel crunchy under their feet. 'We'll explore it later, but first we'll find a place to eat,' said Mary, leading them round the back. Her father smiled as he looked around him. 'Begod, but these monks knew where to live — what?'

The ground sloped to the river and the river curved round the monastery, almost like a moat. There was no shade of any kind, only the long shadows cast by the ruined buildings. They sat down against the wall, glad of the comparative coolness, but feeling the warmth of the old stone against their backs. Mrs. Johnson, despite the fort-

73

night of drought, spread rugs beneath them, and warned them against rheumatism. 'That river is like tinfoil,' said Mr. Johnson, and indeed, it shone so brightly that it hurt your eyes to look at it. Beyond, the land stretched flat and treeless, not a house in sight anywhere. The silence enfolded them, and the low regular murmur from the river only served to emphasise the stillness of the day.

'I wonder could you drink that water? It makes me thirsty just to look at it,' Mr. Johnson asked.

'No water for you today,' replied Mary. 'I've something much better. Now leave it all, Ma, I'll do the unwrapping. This is still part of the surprise, you know. I've gone to a lot of trouble over the picnic — I always think they can be miserable affairs if you don't do them properly.'

As she talked, she began to draw things out from the various bags. The table-cloth was unfolded and spread on the grass. It too caught the sun. 'It looks like a white house in Andalucia,' — Mary had been to Spain the previous summer. Glasses, plates, knives and forks were all spread out. Mrs. Johnson thought that she had never seen a picnic like this before. What were the glasses for? And how did you eat sandwiches with a knife and fork?

'No soggy sandwiches for us,' said Mary, unwrapping a chicken. Then she took out a long package and began to undo it. Layer after layer of paper, cardboard, straw were peeled off, and a slim bottle of wine at last emerged. 'Ice cold,' she said, 'I got the man in the shop to keep it in the fridge till the last minute, and then I insulated it like this myself.' She laughed across at her mother. 'Don't worry, Ma, I didn't forget you.' She took out a flask. 'Tea. Good strong tea, and all for yourself — Daddy and I'll have the wine.' She spread out every-

74

thing on the table-cloth in front of them. The skin of the chicken was brown and crisp and there were red tomatoes and golden oranges and a potato salad in a creamy mayonnaise sauce.

Mary served the three of them. Gratefully, her mother drank some tea. How refreshing tea was on a day like this — much better than any of those cold drinks. And certainly a lot better than wine. Wine always made her thirsty and gave her a headache. But this tea — she could drink the whole flask and no bother. She poured some more into her cup and looked across at her daughter and husband. She didn't want to talk; just to sit there and feel the happiness seeping into her body. She hadn't felt like this for years. All her aches and worries seemed to have disappeared, and sitting there in that green field she felt like a girl again. She lay back in the sunshine. She remembered her own home. She remembered the times she used to bring bottles of tea and currant bread to her father and brothers as they worked on the hay during the long summer days. Sometimes, if the weather had been very bad, she would have to help too, but mostly, with five brothers her father had plenty of labour, and all she had to do was bring the tea out to them at one and again at five. They'd all sit down in the meadow together, with the smell of the new-mown hay drugging their senses. They'd eat and drink and talk a little, and her father would give her a penny sometimes, for all her hard work, as he said. Tea and bread had never tasted the same since. The very taste of the world had changed. Those summer dreams had never been fulfilled; not that she could remember what it was she had dreamt, sitting beside her father and brothers in the sweet-smelling meadow. But she remembered the magic, the surging excitement as the world opened up before her; the aching happiness as she stood on the threshold of adventure and romance.

Foolishness. Such foolishness. The world had not opened up. It had shrunk, until it was encompassed by a small terrace house in the south suburbs of Dublin. Her husband was a man who came home in the evenings, too tired to talk. He sat in his shirt sleeves before the fire and read the evening paper, nodding over it, until at about half nine or ten he would drag himself to bed. This tiredness increased as the years went on, and when he retired from his job, five years ago, she thought he must have lost the habit of speech. And the boys — her two sons, where were they now? She had no idea.

But today the magic had come back. Today, she was a girl again. 'I think I'll get Mary to do my hair for me next week,' she mused. 'And Daddy and myself should go away for a few days when Mary is on holidays. It would do him good. But he looks well — how well he looks today. A handsome man. What a marvellous day.'

'Hey, Ma, wake up. You're miles away from us. Daddy and I are going to rinse these plates out in the river. Your day off. Mustn't do anything at all.' What a strange woman her mother was, always going off into some dream world of her own. Mary remembered even as a child, her mother's eyes would sometimes stop seeing her and she would be off somewhere else. This used to infuriate her — that she couldn't follow where her mother went. But now she liked it. She liked this dream mother who seemed so much younger than herself in many ways. Her mother would always have that vulnerable air about her, she realised, looking back at her

76

sitting there, playing with a blade of grass.

Mary handed her father a plate which she had just rinsed. How he had enjoyed himself today. He reminded her of when she was young, and he would take her to Mass on Sunday, holding her hand tightly, and telling her stories of his own childhood. Her parents. She felt close to them again; today they were a family.

They felt so tired when they began to prepare for the journey home. The sun was still shining, although it was after five o'clock. The car, which Mary had parked in the shade, was cool as they sat into it. What an effort it was to keep one's eyes open, listening to the throb of the engine. 'Hey, Ma,' Mary said, 'say something or I'll fall asleep over the wheel.' But the conversation petered out, as they sat there enjoying the sensation of tired, relaxed bodies, moving imperceptibly with the motion of the car. If only the journey could go on and on forever.

Back in the house, Mrs. Johnson said she would make some more tea for them. 'No thanks,' said Mary, 'I couldn't eat or drink another thing. I think I'll go up to bed, even though it's still early. I can read for a while.' Her mother kissed her. 'Do, Mary,' she said, 'off you go, you must be tired. What a marvellous day. Daddy and I certainly enjoyed ourselves.' She paused. 'You're so good to us, such a good daughter.' Quickly she turned her face away and began to busy herself with the crockery.

Mary didn't say good-night and she didn't look at them. She ran up the narrow stairs and into her room. Closing the door behind her she walked over to the window. The sky was darkening outside and in the distance she thought she could hear the first rumblings of thunder. She placed her car keys on the dressing table and noticed that she was still holding the little posy she had gathered earlier. Wild woodbine and scarlet poppies. Already they were beginning to wither.

Outside, the garden was now in complete darkness. Firmly she drew the curtains together and switched on the light. The day was over.

Aimez-vous Colette?

As I walk to school in the morning, or go for my
groceries at the week-end, or perhaps pay a visit to
the local public library, I often wonder — do I present a figure of fun? I should I suppose: provincial
school-mistress; spinster; wrong side of forty.
Certainly I must seem odd to those pathetic rustic
minds to whom any woman of my age should be
safely wed, or in a nunnery, or decently subdued
by her continuing celibacy. I teach in a convent.
No ordinary convent, mind you, for the nuns are
French, and as you might expect this gives the
school a certain cachet among our local bourgeoisie.
Most of the girls are boarders — day girls are
tolerated with an ill grace — and many of them
spring from quite illustrious lines. The leading
merchant has two daughters here; the doctor and
the dentist three apiece. Even the surgeon in the
County Hospital has sent his Melissa to us.

The town in which I work and live is one of those
awful provincial Irish towns which destroys without
exception anyone of any sensitivity who must live
there. It is every bit as narrow, snobbish and anti-
thought today as it was twenty years ago. It is the
sort of town which depraved Northerners — Swedes,
Dutch and the like — are captivated by. They
always assure us, on departing, that our unique
attitude towards life and our marvellous traditions

must be preserved, at all costs, against encroaching materialism.

As you may have guessed, I do not like this town: neither, however, does it make me unhappy. Unhappiness, I am beginning to realise, is a condition of the young. I realise it more as I spend a whole day — sometimes as much as a week — without being actively unhappy myself. Even those mediocrities who surround me do not upset me excessively any more. At most I occasionally feel something a little sharper than irritation at their absurd attempts at liberalism. Such as collections and fasts outside church doors for the Biafrans, when every mother within twenty miles would lock up her daughter if a black man came to town. And would be encouraged by their priests to do so.

But on the whole, as I said, I live life with a modicum of enjoyment. I have a small house, and a cat. I grow vegetables and flowers and I buy beautiful and expensive clothes in Dublin and London. I cook well, and I enjoy a glass of wine with my meals. I have no friends, but I do not feel the need of them. When I leave the victim daughters of the bourgeoisie behind, having duly carried out my daily efforts at subversion with the help of Keats and Thomas, I return to my little house and close my door on the outside world. Then I read. As Miss Slattery in the Public Library says, I am a terrible reader. I prefer the French to the English novel, and with the best, the most sophisticated and subtle minds for company, why should I care about an Ireland that continues to rot in obscurantism and neurosis?

I particularly like the novels of Colette. I have always been drawn to her work. She creates an ambience which I have never found elsewhere, except in poetry. Indeed I often think that if it were not for Colette, I should have left this wretched place years ago. But her books are so peopled with village school-mistresses, leading romantic and smouldering lives in some distant town, I may foolishly have thought that something similar might happen to me, here in *my* distant Irish town. But Irish towns are not French towns. Or perhaps the whole point is that they are: if I were living deep in the Midi, teaching the daughters of the local bourgeoisie at the local Lycée, I would perhaps find myself surrounded by just such nonsense and stupidity as I do here. It is, after all, the romantic vision of Madame Colette which transforms and enhances.

I have often thought of writing myself. I am sure I could, for I consider myself to be intelligent and perceptive enough and my retired life is ideally suited to such an occupation. I have hours of undisturbed solitude, all the bodily comforts that I need, and a job which if dull is not overtaxing — and yet I have never written. Not a line, not even an elegy for Sitwell, my dear cat, when he died last Spring aged twelve years.

Of course, really, I know perfectly well why I do not write; why I will never write. I have nothing to write about. Now I appreciate that this may seem a lame excuse to many; a writer, they will say, a real writer, can write about anything. Look at Jane Austen. Jane Austen, I notice, is always cited in this context, why I don't know, as she has always seemed to me an excessively sociable person with a myriad human relationships. While, by comparison, I am a hermit. It is true that I work and live among people but my relationships with them are invariably tangential. I never exchange a word

81

with my head-mistress, my girls, my butcher, except in the course of business. And I have lived like this for twenty years. Before that, it is true, there was the odd relationship which may appear to have had slightly more substance: a shadowy involvement with my parents, the occasional girlish exchange during my years at a gloomy and indifferent boarding school. On the whole, however, my life could be said to be arid. But, be assured, I do not use the word pejoratively. I am pleased with this aridity. Just as I like the dryness of my skin. I cannot abide clammy skin — it makes me quite ill to come into contact with. But when my hand brushes my cheek and I feel and hear the dry rasp, I experience something akin to pleasure.

In my entire life there is only one incident about which I could write. No, it was not an incident, it was an interlude — a period of joy. I could write about it with ease, for I recall it often and I remember it still with clarity though its pain is no longer as sharp.

Can you imagine me at twenty? I have always been a plain woman, but whereas nowadays I seldom think of this, even when I look in my mirror, at twenty it was the over-riding factor in my life. At school I had never thought about my looks — I don't think any of us did. Cleverness was what counted, and anyway, nobody who spent nine months of the year in the same greasy gym-frock and washed her hair every two months could have any pretensions to prettiness. And when I left my boarding school and went, clutching my County Council scholarship, to pursue my studies at University in Dublin, my terror was so overwhelming that it blotted out every other sensation from my consciousness. As I stood for the first time in the Great Hall of the College, I literally trembled from head to foot.

Today my most outstanding character trait is probably my independence, but in those days I was like a puppy. I became a slave to anybody who threw me a kind word. Perhaps this is why I dislike dogs so much. I prefer my cats — elegant independent beasts, who stalk off, indifferent to all shows of affection. Every time I see a silly pup, wagging his tail furiously, even when he is being kicked out of the way, I am reminded of myself at twenty.

I was staying at Dominican Hall, where I lived for my four years at University. Initially I was even too shy to have tea with the others in the dining-room and I would buy a bun and an apple and eat them by myself in my bedroom. Then, after about a month, I began to venture downstairs and eventually I became accepted. People came to know my name and they'd nod to me as I crossed the Green. I was even included in the tea-time conversations. I was a good listener, and quite a subtle flatterer (though to be fair to myself, I think it was often genuine admiration on my part). I did not make a close friend, but this new-found camaraderie was quite enough. Then, as I gained confidence, and was known even to timidly initiate a conversation myself, I began to realise that I was finding much of my companions' conversation unintelligible. It was all about boys, love affairs and dating; unknown territory to me. Just as I had never thought about my looks, so I had never thought about boys. But now I did. I even began to notice them as I sat in the lecture halls, and it was easy to see what interested the other girls so greatly. Suddenly I was caught up in the excitement of potential romance, just like all the rest. I stopped thinking of myself as an outsider. I felt I was becoming normal.

I began to pay visits to Woolworths, to buy lipsticks and powder and even a home permanent. I could discuss such purchases with the other girls, even sometimes offer them advice on bargain hunting. I woke up every morning with a feeling of anticipation, and instead of going straight to the library, increasingly I found myself going for coffee and a gossip.

At this stage, the question of boy-friends was largely academic as few of the girls actually had one, but we all talked about them constantly. I believed I was attractive to boys. I think I trusted in the magic properties of the make-up I used and I felt that each time I clumsily applied my morning mask I was being liberated from myself and my inadequacies. Of course I was still too shy to actually look directly at boys, but whenever I had to pass a group of them I felt sure that they were all looking at me.

Eventually it was decided (by whom I cannot now recall) that I should join some of the other girls at the Friday evening student dance. I was overwhelmed. I felt far more nervous than I had ever felt sitting for an examination. But I was determined to go, so I took myself in hand and was ready, painted and coiffured, at the appointed time on the Friday.

I went to three dances before I would allow myself to admit that something was wrong. The first night, I was genuinely puzzled. As the evening wore on I couldn't understand why nobody was asking me to dance. Maybe because I didn't know the place and looked awkward as I blundered around searching for the Ladies. Maybe because these boys only danced with the regulars, the girls who came here every week, and they would have to get used to my face before they asked me. At the end of the night I had convinced myself that there was no need to worry and indeed I was looking forward to the next Friday when I would avoid so many mistakes and would surely emanate a new confidence.

But the following week it was the same story, and the week afterwards. That night when I came home I locked myself in the bathroom and stood in front of the mirror. A heavy, rather stupid-looking face stared back at me. The skin was muddy, the hair dull and limp. Even to my novice eyes the inexpertly applied make-up appeared garish and pathetic. The dress which I had chosen with such care hung in sad folds over my flat bosom. I felt myself blush — a deep blush of shame. What a spectacle I must have made of myself. What a fool I must have looked, standing there with a hopeful, grateful expression on my lumpy face, waiting to be asked to dance.

I think most people, when they look back on their youth, find, or pretend to find, these intense emotions rather amusing. It seems to me that this is just another aspect of the sentimentalisation of youth which is so commonly indulged in in middle age. I know that the misery I experienced that night was far greater than anything I have experienced, or could experience, since.

I left the bathroom and I took my lipstick, my powder and my cheap perfume, made a bundle of them, and threw them over the railings into the bushes in Stephen's Green. I resumed my earlier habits, and returned to my reading in the library, where I kept my eyes firmly downcast in case by chance I should meet the pitying gaze of some of those boys whom I had so beseeched at those dances. I took my tea earlier to make sure of avoiding contact with my friends. They never appeared to miss me, and I suppose they were relieved to be rid of someone whom they had tolerated only out of kindness. How had I ever imagined that I could fit in amidst their gay and careless chatter — I, who carried around with me a smell of deprivation and humility which singled me out from these confident grocers' daughters?

I became a most serious student, and it was in this period of my life that I developed my taste for vicarious living. I did not have to totally relinquish my world of romance, for now I found it in the pages of Flaubert, and Hardy and Stendhal.

After a time I became less actively unhappy, and once I could close my door on the world at night I knew peace. I was no longer tormented by my ugliness and ineptitude — there was nobody there to sneer at my clumsy attempts at man-catching — and my antidote against loneliness continued to give me solace as I read late into the night. But with the coming of Spring and the longer evenings, I began to feel restless. An animal stirring perhaps? I found myself gazing around the library, day-dreaming, instead of reading the books lying in front of me. It was in this manner, one day, that I first noticed Humphrey. I was toying with a pencil, idly thinking of nothing, when it rolled away from me across the table. As I retrieved it, again idly, I happened to glance at the man sitting opposite. He had been staring at me, but quickly looked away. It must have been the embarrassment with which he looked away that first aroused my interest, for after that I noticed him practically every day, and he always seemed to find a seat near mine. Sometimes I would catch him gazing at me; at other times he would be totally involved in his work.

At this period there were quite a number of African students at the University, but I think Humphrey was the blackest man I had ever seen. He was quite small, with a rather large head covered in fuzzy down, and long, curiously flat arms. He seemed very ugly to me, but I was flattered by his obvious interest in me and I had all sorts of fiercely-held liberal attitudes which must have affected my reaction towards him. I pitied him too, for I thought that anyone who could find me an object of interest must be desperate indeed.

Soon, when I found him looking at me I would look back, not quite smiling, but in a reasonably friendly manner. I took to saying 'Excuse me,' vaguely in his direction when I left the table. Then one day we literally bumped into each other outside the library door and both of us involuntarily said hello. After this we always exchanged greetings and then about a month later as we sat working I found a note pushed across the table towards me. It read (and I still remember the wording clearly): 'Dear Miss, would you care to break into your morning studies and refresh yourself with a cup of coffee?'

We were soon meeting regularly. As if by agreement, though neither of us ever mentioned it, we never met outside, and we never went anywhere. But every Saturday afternoon at about four o'clock, I would catch the bus to Rathmines, to Humphrey's bed-sittingroom. He lived in a large run-down house, at the top of a hill, just off the Rathmines Road. The house seemed to be let out entirely to African and Indian students, and I can still recall vividly the strong, individual aroma that filled it. It was made up of exotic cooking smells and perspiration and stale perfume. All the other students seemed to entertain their girl-friends on Saturday afternoons too, and I got to know some of them (though we never spoke) as we travelled on the bus or stood on the door-step together. Their approach was either furtive or brazen and I was sure that I was the only undergraduate among them. It made me very angry that these girls should feel that they had to act like this, and also, that these boys should have to have such girlfriends; but when I thought of myself and remembered my own ugliness I was often reminded of a favourite saying of one of the students in Dominican Hall as she prepared for the Friday night dance — 'Any port in a storm.'

Perhaps this was true for me initially, but as I got to know Humphrey I began to realise that he was a person of unusual qualities. He was very gentle — he didn't seem to have any aggression in his make-up at all. He laughed often and easily. He was a cultivated person, and whereas I was a crammer — with my peasant equation: learning equals getting on — he was a scholar.

Each Saturday when I arrived he would very formally shake hands and take my coat and make me comfortable. Then we would sit and talk, I with ease for the first time in my life, discovering too that I could be witty and interesting and that Humphrey obviously thought so. We always listened to music, and I was taught to understand something of its magic. We would sit for hours, listening to string quartets and looking out over the darkening roof-tops. During these periods I grew genuinely to like Humphrey. He seemed so lonely and yet so calm sitting there in the shadowy room. I admired his calm, and my natural kindness and crude radicalism made me suffer what I imagined he was suffering.

Later, when it was quite dark and the light was put on and the spell broken, he would make me a chicken stew. It was of a most spicy, succulent oiliness which I have never tasted since and have never been able to capture in my own cooking. Afterwards he would kiss me and fondle me for half an hour, maybe an hour, and then I'd get up, put on my coat and catch my bus home.

Oh, they were marvellous evenings — oases of brightness in my grey, dull weeks. His kisses healed me, and if they excited him, I never knew. I was too young, too unconscious, for the relationship to have been a sexual one, even in texture. And I am so glad now that I was unschooled in the sex-manuals with their crude theories of the potency of the black man. Our relationship was a relationship of love.

I had never in my life been given a present, not even by my parents who were too busy struggling to keep me at school to have been able to pay for presents. Now Humphrey gave them to me. He would suddenly present me with a flower, or a hairband, or a book. He taught me to open myself, he told me I was pretty, and while I was with him I believed it, for I knew by the way he looked at me that *he* believed it. Most of the time in that bedsitting room, I was happy. I learned to forget myself and my tortured inadequacies.

I don't know how I thought it would end. I knew at the back of my mind that I would not marry Humphrey, but I never really admitted it to myself — I kept it well out of sight and continued to enjoy the present.

Then one Saturday, about three weeks after he had duly carried off a double first in History and Politics, Humphrey handed me a large white envelope as I came in the door. It was an invitation to any of Mr. Ozookwe's friends to the forthcoming conferring ceremonies, and afterwards, to a cup of tea with the President of the College.

'Well,' said Humphrey, 'we'll buy you a new hat. I know exactly the kind you should wear . . .'

This was a shock — I had never thought of it. Not once. I began to feel sick. I thought of all those girls in Dominican Hall, and all the boys who had ignored me at those Friday night dances. I thought of me in my finery, and their comments and their sneers. So this was all I could produce. This was where I ended up. Humphrey was no longer my kind, gentle friend — he was a black man.

'Humphrey, no,' I said, 'you know how I hate social occasions. I won't even go to my own conferring — if I ever get that far.' The little joke could not disguise the panic in my voice. 'I'll tell you what — afterwards, we could . . .' but the expression on his face stopped me. He looked as if he was in physical pain. But his voice was gentle when he spoke.

'Yes, I see,' he said. 'I should have seen all along — it was stupid of me. I am sorry for embarrassing you. I think you'd better go now, please.'

Well, of course, I changed my mind the next day. Humphrey would be going away, it was the least I could do for him, give him this. I would miss him. I would sorrow after him.

I wrote to him but he did not reply. I called at his house, and the second time an Indian answered the door and told me that he had moved, left no address. I never saw him again. He may have been killed in the Biafran War (he was an Ibo), or he may be rich and prosperous, living somewhere in Nigeria, with several wives perhaps. I hope, do you think, that he has forgotten me?

Growth

When Catherine had placed her suitcase, modestly, in the very corner of the overhead rack and stowed her hold-all under her seat, she sat down by the window and looked at her watch. It was half-past eight — the train wasn't due to leave for another hour.

She stood up again, looked out the window, then into the corridor, and then began to inspect the carriage. She examined the sepia print of some ski-resort, the commands in various languages. She ran her hand over the plastic letters, 'Défense de cracher', and, putting her head back, sniffed the air thinly through pinched nostrils. That foreign smell, that, more than anything, made her realize that she was indeed abroad.

She had first stepped onto French soil at the Gare du Nord — at Calais there had merely been Customs sheds, which hardly counted — and from there had gone by Metro to Gare de l'Est to catch her train to Geneva. Her parents had advised her to take a taxi, but she couldn't face the ordeal of trying to make a taxi-driver understand even her simple directions. And what if he deliberately took her the longest way there and she didn't have enough money to pay when she arrived?

Inside the Metro she had found it very difficult to look out for the names of stations, so engrossed was she by the faces all around her. The nonchalance and total self-absorption of these Parisians fascinated her. Every one of them seemed handsome; even the old and the dowdy achieved an air of distinction and sophistication with that marvellous, superior lack of interest.

Now, safely installed in her railway carriage, Catherine looked at her reflection in the window and tried to arrange her features in the same lines of disinterest. But then she suddenly thought again about her money and passport, and forgetting all about her face she dived into her hold-all to make sure they were still there. That must have been the tenth time she had checked them since getting off the boat at Calais.

Before putting away her bag she arranged her towel and tooth brush and brand new make-up in readiness for the morning and took out her novel and a packet of sandwiches. She undid the grease-proof wrapping and bit into one of the sandwiches. The bread tasted as hard and dry as cement. Guiltily, she re-wrapped them and pushed them into the rubbish box. She should have eaten them on the boat, that was what her mother had intended, but nobody had been eating then and she hadn't wanted to draw attention to herself. Well, it would be her own fault if she arrived in Geneva starving. In fact, she was feeling quite hungry already. She wondered if, after all, she should retrieve the sandwiches.

She started up, but as she did, footsteps began to sound outside. Quickly she sat back and opened her novel, not even trying to find her place. The door was slid back gently, and Catherine, peering over the corner of her book, could glimpse only an outline.

'Vous permettez?'

She looked up. 'Oui.'

As she nodded her head the man who had been standing — tentatively it seemed — on the threshold, walked in, followed by a porter. The latter raised two matching pieces of luggage and placed them over Catherine's head beside her own suitcase. They took up nearly the whole rack. Then he began fussing around, hanging up the man's coat, obviously waiting for a tip.

Catherine looked covertly at her fellow traveller. He was old, up to seventy she thought, and small, as if he had shrunk. Still, there was nothing decrepit about him, with his squared shoulders and smooth, pinkish face. His hair and suit were of a silvery grey, and his pale lemon shirt (with matching handkerchief) and highly polished shoes gave him quite a debonair appearance. His nails, she noticed, were carefully manicured and on his little finger a diamond winked.

Catherine, who often found herself pitying old people, which depressed her, now looked with pleasure at this old man. He could take care of himself alright, she could see that; with his air of distinction and intelligence, he might have been a retired diplomat or important civil servant.

He handed a coin to the porter and sat down opposite her. She watched as he crossed his legs, pulling up his trousers with an elegant little gesture. Then he drew out a cigarette case and held it suspended in front of him. 'Vous permettez?' When Catherine again replied 'Oui', he proferred the case to her. She shook her head and he returned the case smoothly to his pocket.

She noticed his movements, it was as if every bit of him had been well oiled. 'Practice makes perfect' flashed irrelevantly through her head and she found

94

herself giggling. Ashamed, embarrassed, in case he might think she was laughing at him, she raised her eyes directly to meet his. But he was smiling at her, nodding through the cigarette smoke. He moved forward. 'Vous êtes Anglaise — oui?' And he was off at a great rate, leaving Catherine completely lost.

'Pardon,' she interrupted, 'je ne parle pas Francais. Parlez-vous Anglais?'

'Mais non,' and he clapped his hands together and laughed as if it were a huge joke. He shook his head at her, still smiling, and, taking out a handkerchief, touched it to his temples. A whiff of cologne reached Catherine, and she sniffed with delight; smells of cologne and foreign tobacco mingled in the carriage, filling it with that exotic aroma that signified Abroad. Catherine smiled back.

She wished she could speak, say something to him, but as she was struggling with her schoolgirl French the door of the compartment opened again and this time a girl entered. She stood in the middle of the carriage, looking round for somewhere to stow her canvas airlines bag.

The old man stood up to help, only reaching to the girl's chin. She glanced at him, then casually waved him away and with one vigorous and graceful movement swung the bag up on the shelf. Then she sat down beside Catherine, stretched out her long legs and addressed a remark in French — to no one in particular it seemed. The man answered her, and they began a quick exchange, the old man very business-like now, no longer smiling. After a few moments, the girl turned to Catherine.

'You're English, I believe?' she said in an American voice.

'No, Irish, actually.' Catherine was blushing again at finding herself suddenly the centre of attention.

'Irish — why that's marvellous,' she sounded genuinely pleased. 'I'm from Wisconsin. I know a lot of Irish people back home. Gee, that seems a long way away now — I've been over here more than two years.'

'Yes, I was wondering when I heard you speak such good French —'

'Oh, you pick it up in no time.'

Catherine looked at her admiringly. She was very American, big and well-made, with a close-knit muscular body — not muscular with bulging arms and legs but with a rich and supple smoothness that suggested regular exercise and good food. She was burnt all over, a dusky reddish-brown, her skin shining as if polished by the sun, especially her knee-caps, which bore a silky gloss. Catherine wished she could touch them, and she glanced down shamefully at her own rough and pallid flesh. The other's hair hung, long and brown and luxuriant, smooth and shining like the rest of her. Her face was bland, so that the only really noticeable feature was her mouth, which she had painted a bright and brazen red. Her frock was red too, but it was hardly an adornment, merely a sop to convention, a covering for the fine, palpitating body underneath. Catherine knew that she was the most attractive person she had ever seen. She could sit and look at her for hours.

The old man was talking to her again, and after a minute or two the girl turned to Catherine. 'Are you getting a couchette for the night, or have you got one? Monsieur here says he never sleeps on trains, neither do I. But how about you?'

'Oh no, no.' The very idea of trying to find a couchette and struggle again in French filled Catherine with terror, and besides, she was going to

96

do whatever the other two did.

'Good, then let's get to work.'

The American girl stood up and began re-arranging the luggage, spreading it out, placing the old man's coat on one seat, and Catherine's cardigan on another. She smiled at Catherine. 'Now we're set up for a comfortable journey. Anyone comes looking for a seat, we're all full up.'

Fleetingly Catherine imagined unhappy passengers sitting outside in the corridors, spending the night uncomfortably on suitcases, but she dismissed these, the thoughts of a novice traveller. The other girl sat down again. 'Well,' she said, 'I'm Janet and this is Monsieur Dechaud and you're —?'

'Catherine.'

'Glad to know you, Catherine. You going on vacation?'

'Yes, a friend of my aunt invited me, she works in Geneva and she thought it would be a good opportunity for me, for my French. Actually —'

'That sounds real nice. I'm going, you'd never believe it, to buy a watch. Why, this time tomorrow night I'll be heading back for Paris on this very train. Do you think it sounds crazy? But you see, I wanted a really good watch, and you save so much in Switzerland. Besides, I can say I've seen Mont Blanc.'

Well, Catherine had heard of many things, but never anything as glamorous as this. Imagine — travelling all the way to Switzerland to buy a watch. She herself wouldn't dream of going to Cork, never mind London, on such a frivolous errand, and here was this girl . . .

As they hurtled along, but somewhat sedately within the solid comfort of their second-class compartment, darkness began to gather outside. What

97

little colour there had been in the countryside was draining away; here and there a light sprang up, white and insubstantial in the twilight.

'Shall we leave the blinds up? It's such fun looking out at night.'

At Janet's words, the three turned and looked together at the bleakening night beyond. Then with relief they turned back and smiled at one another in the cosiness of their glowing carriage.

'We are like a family party,' Catherine thought. 'Anyone looking in and seeing us must imagine Papa and his daughters off to Switzerland for the holidays.' The thought made her feel happy, closer to the other two, who had now resumed a desultory conversation. But the old man was not neglecting her: from time to time he would sign over to her, feign a yawn, raise his eyebrows interrogatively. When she signed back that she too was tired, he would pat her knee, laugh, shake his head at her. He was such a nice old man, and Janet sounded so offhand, almost brusque. Catherine wished that she would take a little more trouble, make some effort to hide her boredom, but even as she condemned her, she couldn't help admiring her. Janet, she imagined, would never try to please anyone, she was too independent for that. You took her as you found her, and if you didn't like her, well, she wouldn't lose any sleep over it.

Catherine closed her eyes and imagined herself like Janet, cool and calm and displaying such fine indifference; sophisticated, that's what she was. 'And that's what I want to be.'

As the night progressed the other two withdrew more into themselves, talked less, grew less alert. Catherine — although her bottom was beginning to ache and her back to stiffen — watched them with unsurfeited fascination. They began a game of poker (which Catherine didn't know how to play) but soon threw it up; Janet took out some French magazines and flicked through them, discarding them one after the other. The compartment was thick with cigarette smoke but the other two didn't seem to notice and kept on lighting cigarettes, long French ones, and stubbing them out after a few puffs.

Nobody had said anything for some time when suddenly the old man stood up and began talking to Janet and pointing to his seat, as if in invitation.

Janet turned to Catherine. 'Sir Galahad here is worried about our comfort.' Catherine hoped he hadn't understood or picked up the irony in the voice. 'He suggests we both stretch out, put up our feet. He doesn't want to — he'll just sit over there at the door and guard us. How about that for a gentlemanly suggestion?'

Catherine was too worried to consider whether it was gentlemanly or not. If she took off her shoes, suppose her feet were smelly? And if she left them on, what would the others think of her uncouthness? However, Janet had now stretched out, and brown toes, bared and unsmelly and uninhibited, were forcing Catherine off the seat. She sat down opposite. The old man, watching her, patted the red plush. 'Up,' he said, 'up,' and obediently she put her feet up. Then he sat down, squeezing himself onto the end of the seat, but when Catherine tried to withdraw her feet to make room for him, he pulled them back and gently re-arranged them together.

'Won't he be very uncomfortable, sitting up all night like that?' Catherine timidly suggested.

'You're doing him a favour, honey — letting him

99

play the gallant. Just you go right to sleep.'

Catherine didn't sleep, didn't want to sleep, but she felt herself being lulled into a trance-like calm by the regular swaying of the train and the distant throb of the engine. Within the carriage, all movement had ceased; nobody seemed even to breathe as they sped through the darkness. It was pleasant to lie there, to let an ever-increasing remoteness creep over you, so that you could almost look in at yourself, see yourself, lying there, suspended in time. Catherine yawned sensuously. 'Even if I tried to worry now, I just couldn't.'

At Dijon the train grumbled to a halt and she heard voices outside, men shouting at one another, as if from a great distance. Then they were off again, moving smoothly into the sleeping countryside. Her companions were silent, motionless; the only light in the carriage came from the dim night lamp overhead. In spite of herself, Catherine dozed off.

She had no idea how long she had been asleep when, suddenly, she was startled into alertness. As she opened her eyes the first blue shadows of dawn were beginning to filter into the compartment and she could feel some weight against her, something pressing her down. She peered up and could make out an outline, a presence that was hovering over her body. Then hands reached out, something brushed her lips and settled on them. With a mixture of fear and revulsion she realised it was the old man. He was kissing her! His lips were dry and paper-like, she could hear them rasping in the silence.

She lay quite still, feeling his lips, and as she did, she found her initial reactions being replaced by curiosity: a man of — what — he must be about

100

seventy and probably a grandfather; she had never realised . . . . she wouldn't have believed . . . .

She allowed his lips to rest on hers for another second or two, but then as she felt his hands begin to move she threw out her arms to fend him off, turned on her side, muttering to herself in feigned sleep. The old man pressed her head once more and then moved away. Catherine opened her eyes a cautious slit — he was back again in his corner, but the seat opposite was vacant. She looked towards the corridor; a cigarette-end was glowing in the darkness and she could just see the outline of a graceful head, cocked — or did she imagine it — at a sardonic angle.

In the morning they sat facing one another again, spruced up in so far as the tiny and by now filthy wash-room had allowed. The other two appeared remarkably well, showing no signs of a sleepless night. Monsieur was still smiling and nodding, Janet had already lit a cigarette. As Catherine looked at the old man, she felt almost a fondness for him. Janet was beautiful, but he had chosen *her* — never mind why. It could be, couldn't it, that he had simply preferred her?

The bustle when they arrived at the station was overwhelming, and before they could even say good-bye properly to Monsieur Dechaud, he had been whisked away by his daughter to her dogs and her villa in Haute Savoie.

Janet turned to Catherine. 'Let's have a coffee together before I go search for my watch.' So together they strolled through the morning sunshine and sat down at the station buffet. Without consulting Catherine, Janet ordered two cafés crême, and lit another cigarette.

'Well, honey,' she said, stretching out her long

101

brown legs, 'I guess you had an interesting night?'

Catherine saw the gleam of anticipation in the other's eye; it was an invitation to intimacy, to shared confidences, and she wanted desperately to accept. But she couldn't, she owed something to that old man.

Steadfastly she looked back at Janet. 'I don't know what you're talking about,' she said, and as she did, she began to sense within her, joyously, a growing feeling of indifference towards this — this heroine. Three countries she had been through since she had left Ireland two days ago. Maybe by the end of the summer her legs would even have turned brown.

A Truly Romantic Soul

For years afterwards, little details from that holiday
would come back suddenly and Elizabeth would
find herself remembering sharply. It happened in
all sorts of odd places — in the bath, at the super-
market, as she read her magazine in the launderette.
With uncharacteristic clarity those ten days pursued
her, haunted her, even when Timmie's face itself
had become indistinct and only the boyish outline
remained. She decided that it was guilt and because
she lived with a permanent though undefined sense
of guilt anyway, she felt that she owed a certain
respect to the genuine article, and so after a while
she ceased to put it away but came to terms with
it, her albatross.

They had gone to Kerry because a friend of
Timmie's had offered him a house there, and
because neither of them had had a holiday that
summer and because it was such a marvellous
September. They had seldom spent a holiday together — in fact, this was only their second in the
four years of their relationship. There had been
week-ends, particularly in the early days, snatched
here and there in rural hotels, as they motored
madly from one province to the next, exhilarated
by the idea of hopping in and out of strange beds
and breakfasting wickedly naked under strange
sheets as the country-girl waitress stood awkwardly

by with coffee and toast and bacon.

But by this time, a holiday with Timmie held no appeal for Elizabeth. She wished she could think of some way of getting out of it, but it didn't seem possible without hurting him dreadfully, and anyway, she felt that she really ought to leave him this memory — a sort of goodbye gift that he could always look back on and treasure. But how could she bear Timmie, twenty four hours a day, seven days a week? He would be there, doggedly devoted; she could imagine him, even in his sleep, calling her name, rooting for her hand. In Dublin, she was at least protected by her job and their friends, but in Kerry there would be nothing, nobody to come decently between them, to allow her to breathe.

However, she knew she would go in the end. She owed it to Timmie. She would go and she would be kind and sweet-tempered and do everything that he wanted them to do. It was such a shame that their relationship was breaking up — it saddened her to think of it. He had been her first real boyfriend and that must mean something to a girl. Of course, there had been other *men* — she was, after all, twenty-three when the friendship had begun. There had been sexual experiments, and romantic, impossible boys — married men, a negro student, an ex-farm-labourer turned folk singer. They had come and they had gone, but Timmie had been the first one whom she could have seriously contemplated marrying.

Elizabeth had always seen herself as a nonconformist, an arty, Bohemian sort of creature. She shunned the conventions, loathed everything bourgeois and firmly believed in socialism and the millenium. But secretly, deep in her most private recesses, she had a sneaking admiration for the

104

middle classes. She admired their assurance and air of capability, of knowing where they were going. She supposed herself to have been born somewhere on the fringes of this class, but nevertheless, she was terrified by it. She only had to hear a certain nuance in a voice, a certain emphasis in a sentence, a reference to lavatory rather than toilet, and she found herself utterly vanquished. She stood gauche, poise fled, clownish charm dissipated, air of indifferent nonchalance erased.

Thus Elizabeth knew, but hoped that nobody else would ever find out, that the autonomy of her colourful life-style was a fiction. She never chose her beaux — they were the only type of men that it ever seemed possible for her to end up with. But all that had changed with Timmie. Initially, it had been a question of mistaken identity: seeing him at the party, and thinking him to be another of Flora's strays, she had picked her way through the drunks sprawled on the living-room carpet, and charmingly, easily, engaged him in conversation. The advantage was hers — she was used to handling such young men, and when a fortnight later she discovered that Timmie was not at all what he had seemed, that he was in fact a respectable young College lecturer who was living in the suburbs with his parents and hoping for a staff appointment next year, when she discovered all this, they were both too securely in love for it to make any difference. And Timmie, a secret and very shy poet, found in Elizabeth's rather raffish air all the romance which she found in his clean, shining cheeks, smelling faintly of after-shave lotion, and his rather old-fashioned good manners.

Timmie, in fact, was perfection, a man with a soul, a poet who wrote divinely and, at the same time, a man who believed in earning his living, who *wanted* to pay for Elizabeth's drinks, and who furthermore believed in bathing regularly. Indeed they *were* in love — and with the approval of all. Flora commended Elizabeth's choice, as did her mother, who hoped that at last her daughter might be settling down. But despite all this, they did not think of getting married. Elizabeth thought that it would be rather letting the side down to plunge into a straight life so early on, and Timmie was reluctant to force his stuffy conventions on his dear, unconventional Elizabeth. So they pursued their happiness in the single state — dancing, drinking, making love. 'Living', as they put it, smiling fondly at one another.

Then what had gone wrong? Why had Elizabeth grown restless, begun to feel trapped? She had questioned herself sincerely, upset, afraid for Timmie, so obviously still in love. She looked at him and found him still unchanged — good-looking, gentle, thinking only of her. But these very qualities which had so captivated her originally, now began to exasperate her. She thought it had something to do with not being married. If she *were* married, she wouldn't think about their relationship and Timmie so often. She would just accept things as wives did. She had been grateful and surprised when Timmie had fallen in love with her, but three years of being constantly adored had built up her ego, so that now she felt like trying her luck again. She'd see a man looking at her and feel, yes, I could have him — he fancies me. But at the same time there seemed nothing for it but to stick it out. She drifted along in the relationship and supposed that the drift would eventually carry her into marriage. She was frightened at the idea, but she could see no alternative. Certainly not confronting Timmie, breaking his heart.

And she probably would have married Timmie, if it hadn't been for Chris. Chris, small, ugly, and aggressive, and Timmie's first cousin. 'I'm mad about you, you silly wench,' he said the second time they met, as he reached to embrace her under Timmie's father's stunted apple trees. 'What in God's name are you doing, hanging around with that stick Timmie? Leave him — come back to L.A. with me. I'll be there for another couple of years, you'd love it.'

Elizabeth felt the skin of her back, crushed against the rough bark of the tree, but she was happy, she could breathe again. Chris was hypnotizing her, forcing her to free herself from Timmie. A week later the struggle with her conscience was over, but she remembered her commitments. 'I must go to Kerry with him,' she explained to Chris. 'Timmie's been very good to me and I owe him something, one last happy memory. And I can tell him about us then too.'

It was a perfect September. The sun shone every day, but because the children had gone back to school they had the beaches and the parched brown mountains to themselves. They bathed lazily and afterwards ate gritty sandwiches on the sand dunes. They went for walks on quiet, deserted roads, and turned off into fields to make love while the cows chewed on, unmoved. At night they sat in country hotel dining-rooms and ate thick juicy steaks served with strong tea and slabs of bread and butter. On twilight evenings they stood beside mountain streams, fishing for trout, catching nothing, walking slowly afterwards to the pub for a final whiskey before going to bed.

It was details like these that Elizabeth remembered afterwards. All the smells and tastes and bright sunlit sights kept coming back to her with a tangy vividness. She had to try very hard to remember how unhappy she had been. Timmie was inescapable: even when she locked herself in the bathroom, she could feel his love oozing all over, tacky. If she woke up at night she found his leg or his arm stuck to her, cemented there with sweat. She longed for the coolness of her own bed, or better still, for Chris's hard, leathery skin. She was sure Chris never perspired. She was worried, too, about telling Timmie. She had decided on the last day — that seemed best, when there would be no time left for scenes and recriminations. But how should she do it? Should she make an occasion of it and cook a dinner in the little house and tell him over the wine and candles? Or would it be better to keep it very simple? In the end, she lost her nerve and did neither. She kept putting it off, and it wasn't until they were back in Dublin and Timmie was busy with the rush-hour traffic that she forced the words out.

'Timmie — I have to tell you now. You've been marvellous, but I'm afraid it has to end here. I know I'm awful, I know you can never forgive me, I can't forgive myself, but I can't help it. I just can't go on.'

When she thought about it years later, that seemed to Elizabeth the last vivid memory she ever retained. Her marriage to Chris, her life with him in California, her divorce, all blurred into indistinction, but still she could recall sharply Timmie's white face, his Adam's apple zooming crazily up and down as she told him that she no longer loved him.

The divorce she had taken in her stride — in fact it seemed to suit her. Chris was very decent about the alimony and she had no regrets about leaving California, or Chris and his new teenage playmate. She moved to New York and then to London. She liked London and spent five years there but she always felt restless and she knew there was only one thing for it — she must return to Dublin.

Dublin hadn't changed at all and she seemed to take up exactly where she had left off thirteen years before. The bedsitter which she found for herself was larger than the original but still on the shabby side; the parties she soon began going to (there was no question of an invitation, one just went) were any of them the same as the one where she had met Timmie. She considered that she herself had gained. Hers was the sort of face that mysteriously improves with wear and tear and her air of rather vague sadness was most becoming. She wasn't particularly interested in the young men who brought her sticky glasses of wine and afterwards took her home, telling her how beautiful she was as they sighed and shuddered in the cold dawn hours, looking for some kind of comfort in her little bed. But she always thought of Timmie, and as she smoothed a brown head or a blond and murmured, 'Hush, now darling, quiet,' it was Timmie's head she was caressing, Timmie's spirit she was soothing.

As she thought about her life, she felt that she was that sort of woman who was enjoying her middle-age as she had never enjoyed her youth. She was independent, in fact quite well off — Californian alimony saw to that. She was at ease with herself, anchored, able to suck out such daily pleasure as came her way. True, she had few friends, and her family had disowned her since the divorce, but although she had always felt a great need of other people, Timmie seemed to supply this need now. The young men came and the young men went, but he was permanently there, she could rely on him. She wondered what he must be like now; she hoped he had retained his good looks — so many people lost them when they suffered as Timmie had. But though she occasionally thought of his contemporary self, what warmed her, what she liked to recall, was the Timmie of twenty years ago. She had no desire to see him again, she was very comfortable with her memories.

And then they did meet, literally bumped into each other. Rushing to get some money from her bank — for she was already late for the hairdresser's — she cannoned into a tall man standing at the teller's counter. Her bag went flying, its contents scattering over the marble slabs, and as she bent to retrieve them the man moved over to assist her. They were both kneeling, both mumbling mutual apologies, when he suddenly stopped, lipstick case poised in mid-air. 'But it's — no, it can't be. After all these years — is it really — Elizabeth?'

He had recognised her all right, though Elizabeth didn't think she would have recognised him. This man was a stranger — a thickening, prosperous, forty-year old. But what was it that she noticed instantly, that she had been vaguely trying to identify, even before he had spoken? She knew — it was his smell, his own dear smell. That special mixture of tobacco and whatever soap he used. She smiled up at him, reassured — it was the old Timmie.

He had retained his diffidence too. 'Shall we — are you in a hurry? We must — wouldn't you like a drink or a coffee or something?'

He guided her out of the bank and into a nearby

110

hotel. She fled to the Ladies. She could feel herself trembling, she would have to control herself. Fearfully she looked at her reflection under the fluorescent glare, but she didn't have to worry, she looked quite well. She applied more lipstick, tidying the corners of her mouth carefully, and resettling her beret at a jaunty angle.

Back in the bar, Timmie had bought them both gin-and-bitters. Elizabeth felt herself beginning to tremble again. He had remembered — that was always what she drank, and she had introduced him to it. She looked at his face, she wanted to touch him, it was as if they had been separated only for a couple of hours. She could hear his voice at a distance, dimly, but she didn't want to listen to the words. She could feel herself expanding, uncurling, as a cat does in the sun. But he had paused now, was looking at her expectantly, obviously awaiting some kind of answer.

'Yes, my dear,' she said with meaning. She hoped he would pick up the nuance. It was yes from now on as far as she was concerned.

'That must be why we never met, I suppose. Since we moved to Cork I'm rarely in Dublin.' We, what did he mean by we? 'It was marvellous luck that we should have bumped into one another like that. Look, Elizabeth, you must stay and have lunch. My wife will be back shortly. I want you to meet the whole family. Would you believe it — my eldest boy is nearly seventeen?'

On the bus home she began to feel quite ill. It was the sense of betrayal which was affecting her most of all. Imagine — a seventeen year old son. She must barely have had her back turned when he was off with someone else. While she had been devoting herself to him and his memory, had been giving him the best years of her life. The sorrow tightened round her heart. She would never recover, she knew that for a certainty. She would wait quietly, a lonely old woman, until death took her, a happy release.

As she sat there, nursing her grief, words came back to her, words from her school days. 'And thy heart one day a sword shall pierce.' Words spoken by Simeon to Our Lady in the Temple. What she had to suffer, what she had to go through. Women were made for suffering, perhaps. Our Lady of Sorrows. And she had turned her back on her too. She had forgotten all the teachings of her youth, the love of Jesus, and His Mother. Why had she turned away from her real and only love? Why had she settled for mere men when Jesus was offering her Eternal Love? She remembered, mistily, scenes from her childhood, the warmth of belonging. She sighed voluptuously.

By the time she was turning the key in her hall door, a faint smile was playing round her mouth, and that air of vague sadness, which so became her, had settled round her once again.

Such Good Friends

Although it all happened over two years ago, I still cannot think about Edith without pain. My husband tells me I am being silly and that I should have got over it long ago. He says my attitude is one of self-indulgence and dramatisation and that it is typical of me to over-react in this way. I have told no one but Anthony, and I think that this is a measure of the hurt I suffered, not to be able even to mention it to anyone else. I don't think I am over-reacting — though I admit that I have a tendency to get very excited when I discover a new friend or a potential friend. This may sound as if I am wallowing in permanent adolescence, but even if this were so, the knowledge still wouldn't stop me being overcome with joy if I should meet someone whom I felt to be truly sympathetic.

It may be that I feel like this because I have had so few real friends in my life. I do not say this with any suggestion of self-pity; I am aware that such affinity of spirit is a very rare commodity and so, when there is a possibility of finding it, why, there is every reason to be excited. And it is something I have only ever found with members of my own sex.

Not that I have ever had any shortage of men friends. I have a certain bold physical appeal which seems to attract them, and before I was married, I always had four or five men hovering around, waiting to take me out. I don't deny that this gave me a satisfaction — it was sexually stimulating and very good for one's ego — but I have never felt the possibility of a really close relationship with any of these men. Even Anthony, to whom I have been married for five years, and of whom I am genuinely fond, even he spends half the time not knowing what I am talking about, and indeed, I am the same with him. Men on the whole are unsubtle creatures. You feed them, bed them, and bolster their egoes, and they are quite content. They demand nothing more from a relationship, and for them physical intimacy is the only kind that matters. They don't seem to feel a need for this inner communion, they are happy to jog along as long as their bodies are at ease. I do not bare my soul to men. I tried to once with Anthony in the early days of our marriage, and, poor dear, he became upset and was convinced that I must be pregnant. Pregnant women are known to suffer from all sorts of strange whims.

You may by now think that I do not like men, but you would be quite wrong. I do like them and I am sure that living with one must be so much easier than living with a member of one's own sex. They are easy to please, and easy to deceive, and it is on the whole therapeutic to spend one's days and nights with someone who sees life as an uncomplicated game of golf, with the odd rough moments in the bunker. All I point out are their limitations, and I do so knowing that these views may be nothing more than an eccentricity on my part.

However, to return to Edith. I first met her during a bomb scare when that spate of bomb scares was going on, a little over two years ago. Before my marriage I had been studying law. I passed my first two exams and then I left to get married. About a year later I decided I would try to get a job as a solicitor's clerk, for I found I was bored doing nothing all day long and I thought it might be a good idea to keep my hand in, so to speak. It would make it easier if I ever decided to go back to College and attempt to qualify.

The firm where I got my job had its offices on the top floor of an old house in Westmoreland Street. The offices had a Dickensian air of shabbiness and dust, although I knew the firm to be a thriving one. It consisted of Mr Kelly Senior, Mr Kelly Junior, and Mr Brown. Along with five typists and myself of course. Mr Brown was a down-trodden man of the people, who was particularly grateful to Mr Kelly Senior for having lifted him from the lowly status of clerk to the heights of a fully fledged solicitor. He spent his days trotting round after the boss, wringing his hands and looking worried, and, as far as I could see, making a general nuisance of himself. Mr Kelly *pere et fils* were tall dour Knights of Columbanus. They had crafty grey eyes in emaciated grey faces and they always dressed in clerical grey three piece suits. One day, Mr Kelly *fils* caused quite a sensation when he ventured in wearing a yellow striped shirt, but this break with tradition must not have met with approval, for next day, and thereafter, he was back to the regulation policeman's blue.

The typists in the office were nice girls. I had little to do with them, as I had my own room, and only saw one of them when I had any work to give to her. In the beginning, as I was the only other female in the office, I did try joining them for morning coffee. However, it was not a success. They were not at their ease, and neither was I. I didn't know what to say to them, and they were obviously waiting for

115

me to leave until they could resume their chatter of boyfriends and dances and pop music. There was only about six years difference in our ages, yet I felt like another generation. It was because of this lack of contact that I hardly noticed Edith's existence, although she had been in the office nearly six weeks. That was, until the day of the bomb scare.

We were cursed with bomb scares that winter and particularly irritated by this one, the third in the same week. We filed out of the building, silently, as people were doing on either side of us. The novelty had worn off and these regular sorties into the winter afternoons were beginning to get under people's skin. It was bitterly cold, and I thought I might as well go and have a drink. It seemed more sensible than standing around in the raw air, making small talk. I crossed over the bridge and turned down towards a little pub that I had discovered on such a previous occasion. I sat sipping a hot whiskey, enjoying the muggy warmth, when I happened to glance across at the girl sitting opposite me. She looked familiar in some vague way, and just as I was wondering if she was from the office, she caught my glance and smiled back at me. Yes, now I remembered, she was one of the typists alright, and now that she had seen me I felt obliged to go over and join her. I hadn't wanted to — I had been looking forward to a nice quiet drink without the effort of conversation. But I couldn't be so obviously rude.

'You're with Kelly and Brown,' I began, sitting down beside her.

Her smile was diffident, almost frightened.

'Yes, that's right. And you're Mrs. Herbert. I know because the other girls told me — I haven't been long there myself. My name is Edith Duggan,' she added and held out her hand, rather formally I thought. We sat side by side, both of us ill-at-ease. I was wondering what I could talk about, and then I saw, lying open in front of her, a copy of *The Great Gatsby*. Good — at least this could be a common theme.

'Please call me Helen,' I said. 'Any friend of Gatsby's is a friend of mine. Do you like Scott Fitzgerald?'

'Oh I love him, I think he's great. He's marvellous.'

Her whole face lit up, and it was then I realized what a good-looking girl she was. As I have mentioned before, I have a certain showy attractiveness myself. I know I am not basically good-looking, and I depend heavily for effect on my skilful use of paints. But I have red hair and green eyes, and with a bold make-up I am very much the sort of woman that men stop to look at in the street. I could see now that Helen was not at all like this. She was small and slight, with a tiny face half hidden under a heavy weight of dark brown hair. You would pass her by and not look at her, but if you did stop to take a second look you would realize that her features, though small, were exquisitely proportioned, that her skin had a translucent sheen and that her eyes — her eyes were deep and soft and tranquil. I was the one getting all the barman's looks, but I could see at a glance that Edith was much the finer of us. She was such a charming girl too, shy and low spoken, yet with none of the gaucherie and bluster that so often accompany shyness.

But though I was pleased by her good looks and her charm, it was not these that excited me. What excited me was a realization that here was someone to whom I could speak. Right from the beginning, from my remark about Fitzgerald, I think we both were aware that we were instantly communicating. We talked that day, long into the afternoon, and the more we talked the more we found we wanted to say. It was not only that we shared values and views and interests, but there was a recognition, on both our parts I thought, of an inner identification, a oneness. I knew that I would never have to pretend to Edith, that she would always understand what I was trying to say. I knew that a bond and a sympathy had been established between us and that I could look forward with joy to the times that we would talk and laugh and cry together. I had found a friend.

Do women love their husbands, I sometimes wonder? Do I love Anthony? I know that I like him, that I am grateful to him, that I feel the constant desire to protect him. But love? How can you love somebody you are so apart from? We live together comfortably, but so distinctly. Anthony wants it so, although if I told him this he would be incredulous. I have come to realise as I lie in bed at night, or at the first light of dawn, with his supple body, wracked by pleasure, lying in my arms, that Anthony is undergoing his most profound experience. His body shudders, and his isolation is complete. Sometimes I am amazed by the exclusivity of his passion, although I know well that this sort of pleasure is something that you cannot share. I know, for I am no stranger to pleasure myself; I have felt a tingling in the loins, a heat in the bowels. But I have always kept a weather eye out and asked — is there nothing more? Anthony's capitulation to his body is so complete, and his gratitude to me afterwards so overwhelming, that I know that, for him, this is where we touch, this is where he reaches me. And I am left in the cold outside.

But not once I had met Edith. Anthony should have been grateful to Edith, for with her coming I stopped harrassing him. He didn't have to watch me in the evenings, sitting bleakly in our elegant drawing-room, upsetting his innocent enjoyment of the evening papers. I didn't suddenly snap at him for no reason, or complain of being bored, or depressed, or lonely. Edith became my source of pleasure. Soon we were having lunch together every day, and I would drive her home in the evenings after work. She soon confessed to me that she had been unhappy in the office before she met me, for the other girls were as unwilling to accept her as they had been me, although in both instances, to be fair, I think it was a sensible recognition on the typists' part of our essential difference. We just had nothing to share with them.

For a start, she was older than they were. She had been a third year philosophy student at the University, she told me. A most successful student, apparently, who had hoped to pursue an academic career. She had been working away quite happily, looking forward to her finals, when one day her mother, who had gone quite innocently in search of matches, had found a packet of contraceptive pills in Edith's handbag. It was not, Edith told me, the implication that she was sleeping with a man or men that had so shocked her parents. It was the deliberateness of the act. Young girls did from time to time fall from grace, and it was wrong and they should be punished accordingly. But that anyone, particularly a daughter whom they had reared so carefully, could arm herself with these pills before-

119

hand — that sort of calculation denoted a wickedness and evil of a far more serious order. She was thrown out of the house that very evening and told never to darken the door again.

'The thing I regret most,' Edith said, 'was hurting them. You cannot expect them to understand, the way they were brought up themselves. It's natural that they'd react like that. But I do love them, and I really didn't want to cause them pain. They'll come round, I'm sure. I'll just have to give them a few months, and then everything will be alright I hope. I'll just have to be a lot more careful. But I do miss them, you know — particularly Mammy.'

I had known Edith about six weeks when she introduced me to Declan. She had mentioned him several times, and I gathered that they intended to get married as soon as Declan qualified. He was an engineering student. What a surprise I got the first time I saw him. I couldn't understand, and never did understand afterwards, how someone of Edith's delicacy and intelligence could fall in love with such a slob. And he *was* a slob, a lumbering six-foot-two, with a red face and a slack mouth and a good-humoured, apparently unlimited amount of self-confidence. The night I met him, he had come round after work to collect Edith, and she asked me to stay and have a drink with them. He took us to a rather draughty and gloomy pub, and having bought our drinks, sat opposite me and fixed me with a disapproving eye.

'What,' he asked, 'do you think of the situation in South Africa?'

I later discovered that being a swimming champion all through his school days and most of his college days, Declan had come late to the world of ideas. But not at all abashed by his late start, he was now determined, it appeared, to make up for lost time. I found his zeal rather wearying, I must admit, and I resented the off-hand way he dismissed Edith's comments. I wondered what would happen when he discovered Women's Lib. With a bit of luck he might offer to liberate Edith by refusing to marry her.

In the meantime I realized that Edith would not take kindly to any criticism I might voice and that I had better be careful to simulate some sort of enthusiasm. So next day when she asked me what I thought, I told her I found him very interesting, and that I'd like them both to come to dinner soon and meet Anthony. We decided on the next night, and I said I'd come and collect them as Declan didn't have a car. I planned my dinner carefully and told Anthony to provide an exceptional claret — it was a special occasion. At these times, I'm pleased to be married to a wine merchant, for Anthony can produce the most miraculous bottles, guaranteed to revive any social disaster. I did want Edith to be happy, to like my home and my dinner and my husband. I didn't want to impress her — I knew anyway that the trappings of wealth would leave her unmoved — but I wanted to offer her something, to share whatever I had with her. I was afraid she might be bored.

But I needn't have worried. The evening was a tremendous success and Anthony and Declan seemed to take to one another straight away. Anthony is a most tolerant man, and cannot understand my own violent reactions towards people. I don't think he notices them very much. Once he has had a good meal and with a decent cigar in his hand, he is prepared to listen to all kinds of nonsense all night long. I was amused that evening at the interest he seemed to be showing in Declan's lengthy monologues, nodding his head intelligently and throwing in a 'Really — how interesting' every now and again. Afterwards he told me he thought Declan a 'rather solemn but quite decent chap.'

I blessed his tolerance that night, for I thought it might provide a solution to a problem I saw looming. I had no interest in being lectured to by Declan, and on the other hand, if I saw as much of Edith as I wanted to, if I could take her to films, concerts, even perhaps on holiday, then I knew Declan would begin to resent me and feel perhaps that I was monopolising Edith. But if I could manage to arrange these foursomes, then Anthony would keep Declan happy, and I would have Edith to myself.

And how happy I was at this prospect. The more I saw of Edith, the more I admired and loved her. She had a quietness and repose about her which I found particulary attractive — I am such a strident person myself. I always look for the limelight and though I have tried to cure myself of this fault, I know I am as bad as ever. But Edith actually preferred to listen. And when she listened, you knew that she was actually considering what you were saying, and not simply waiting for an opportunity to get in herself. I talked a lot to Edith, more, I think, than I have ever talked to anyone in my life. The pleasure I got from our conversation was enormous. The world suddenly seemed to be full of things and people and ideas to discuss. I asked for no other stimulant than the excitement generated by our talk, and I looked forward to our meetings with a sense of exhilaration. I loved to buy things for her too. I have always liked giving people

122

gifts, but through being married to Anthony my sense of pleasure had become dulled. Mind you, I don't think it was Anthony, most men would be the same. You can buy a man only a certain number of shirts, and after that — what is there? But with Edith the possibilities were endless. She dressed quite badly — I don't think she ever thought about the way she looked. But I, who saw all the possibilities of her beauty, felt like a creator when I thought of dressing her. A scarf to bring out the purity of her skin, a chiffon blouse to emphasize that fragile line of her neck — the changes I could make in her appearance! Of course I had to be careful not to offend her, as I knew that one so sensitive might be made to feel uncomfortable by all these gifts. So sometimes I would pretend that I had bought something for myself and it didn't fit and she would be doing me a favour by taking it. Or I would accept a pound for a leather bag which had cost me fifteen, saying that I had picked it up cheaply but that the colour wasn't right.

Creating this new Edith re-awoke all my interest in clothes and make-up. I seemed to have been dressing myself and putting on my face for so long that I felt I could do it in my sleep, and I had some time ago grown bored with myself. Besides, presenting my rather obvious persona to the world was a straightforward task, and the subtleties which I used in dressing Edith would have been lost on me. And as Edith saw her new self emerging, she grew interested too. I wondered how this would affect her attitude towards Declan. As she began to realize what a beautiful girl she was, might she not also realize what a slob Declan was, and get rid of him? Not that I thought very much about Declan any more. He was by now busy preparing for his final examinations and when he did have time to go out with Edith he seemed quite happy for them to come and have dinner with us, or at Anthony's club. Anthony had even interested him in wine, and as they sat sniffing their glasses and delicately tasting, we sat giggling over ours, having quaffed too much of the stuff in a most unconnoisseur-like fashion. Edith and I both agreed that we knew little about wine, but knew what we liked. Sometimes, when Declan was studying, I'd go round to Edith's flat for supper, and we'd get through a bottle of plonk enjoying it just as much as any rare Burgundy. This formed a bond between us and gave us a nice comfortable sense of vulgarity, of which Declan would have disapproved for intellectual reasons and Anthony for social.

I was happy. It is a state you have to be in to recognise. Before I met Edith, it had never occurred to me that I was unhappy. I knew that I was bored a lot of the time and often lonely. I felt that something was missing from my life and various well-meaning girl friends had told me from time to time that what I wanted was a baby. Instinctively I knew however that this was not so. I have always rebelled at the idea of becoming a mother; I could never see myself, baby at breast, looking out placidly at the world. Now I knew that my reservations had been right: I would probably have made a very bad mother, and I would not have fulfilled myself. All I needed all that time was a friend. A real friend.

But it seems to be a rule of life that, having achieved a measure of happiness, clouds begin to float across one's Eden. I don't know when things started going wrong with Edith and myself, for my state of happiness had begun to blur my perceptions, and I wasn't as conscious as I should have been of all Edith's reactions. Then little by little I noticed changes in her. She started to make excuses about not coming out to the house with me. When I'd ask her to go to a concert or lecture she'd say no thank you, she was doing something else. She grew irritable too, and would cut me off short when I'd begin to talk about something. Then she took to avoiding me in the office or so it seemed to me, and she started bringing sandwiches in at lunch time, saying that she had no time to go out to lunch as she was doing extra work for Mr Kelly.

When I was certain that I had not been imagining Edith's attitude, when I could no longer fool myself that everything was as it had been, I grew very upset. What upset me most, I think, was that I could not offer an explanation for her behaviour. I knew I was not the most tactful person in the world, but I had felt that Edith and I were so close that there was no need for pretence; and anyway I couldn't remember having said anything so awful that she would stop wanting to see me because of it.

One afternoon I became so worried that I burst into tears in the office. Mr Kelly junior was with me at the time, and I think I frightened the poor man out of his wits, for he told me that I looked tired and to go home at once and not to bother coming in the next day, which was Friday. That week-end I did a lot of thinking. Away from the office I grew calm, and I began to think that things would sort themselves out if I could remain calm. Maybe I had been seeing too much of Edith, and if I left her alone for a while she would probably recover her equilibrium and everything would be alright again.

When I returned to the office, I stuck to my resolution. I remained perfectly friendly towards Edith, but I stopped asking her to come places

125

with me, and I began to have my lunch half-an-hour earlier than the rest of the office. It was so difficult, this calm indifference, but I knew it was the only way. Then one morning as I was taking my coat off, one of the typists rushed into my room.

'Isn't it awful, have you heard?' she said.

'No, what is it, what's happened?'

'Edith Duggan's mother was killed last night. Run over by a bus as she was crossing the road. She died instantly. Edith, the poor thing, went to bits, I believe. They couldn't get her to stop crying.'

God, how awful. I felt quite sick. What must Edith be feeling? I knew she had loved her mother ... and that she should have been killed before they could be reconciled ... The guilt she must be feeling, added to the pain. I must go to her, I knew. I put my coat back on and got her home address from one of the girls, and left without even telling Mr Kelly where I was going.

The house was a shabby semi-detached with a few sad flowers struggling for life in the patch of green outside. A man I took to be Edith's father answered the door. He showed me in to the little front room and there I saw Edith, sitting white-faced and stiff, staring at nothing. She looked up and gave me a wintry smile.

'Edith, what can I say—' I began, but she interrupted me with a shake of her head.

'I know. It's alright really. I understand. It was good of you to come.'

The words sounded so small and distant in that front parlour.

'Oh. Edith, my poor, poor Edith.' I ran towards her and put my arms around her, kissing her, kissing her to comfort her. Suddenly she tore at my arms

126

and flung herself from me. She ran behind the sofa and stood there, trembling.

'Get out of here,' she shouted. 'Leave me alone. Go away you — you monster.'

I tried to say something, but she began to scream some incoherent phrases about the girls in the office and how stupid she'd been and how could I have come there then. I could still hear the screams as I made my way down the path.

She didn't come back to the office. Anthony suggested that she had probably been reconciled with her father and was now staying at home to mind the family. I worried about her, for it seemed to me that the shock of her mother's death must have unhinged her mind. How else could I explain the dreadful things she shouted that day in her front room?

Then about a month later, as I was walking down Grafton Street one afternoon, I saw her coming towards me. She saw me too, and as we drew level I put out my hand. She looked at me, directly into my eyes, with a cold hostility.

'Hello Helen,' she said, and she sounded quite calm. 'I'm glad I've met you like this. You see, I want you to realise that I meant what I said that day. I wasn't hysterical or anything like that. I do not wish to see you ever again.' Then she stepped aside and walked on down towards O'Connell Street.

I felt my stomach heave as she walked away. I felt I could never get home, that I would have to stand there, in Grafton Street, rooted to the spot in horror. I twisted and turned, like an animal in a cage, not wanting to face the fact that Edith's shouted obscenities were the result of no temporary derangement. When I did get home and told Anthony, he refused to discuss it. He said that the only thing to do was to put the whole business out of my mind, forget about it completely. But how could I forget? How can I shrug off the pain and the pleasure, as if it had never happened? I can find no way of doing that, no way of wiping out the profound sense of loss I am left with. You see, we were such good friends, Edith and I. Such good friends.